JULIAN'S MATE

DADDY DRAGON GUARDIANS

MEG RIPLEY

DRAGONS OF CHAROK

Copyright © 2018 by Meg Ripley
www.redlilypublishing.com

All rights reserved. Printed in the United States of America. No part of this book may be used or reproduced in any manner whatsoever without written permission except in the case of brief quotations embodied in critical articles or reviews.

This book is a work of fiction. Names, characters, businesses, organizations, places, events and incidents either are the product of the author's imagination or are used fictitiously. Any resemblance to actual persons, living or dead, events, or locales is entirely coincidental.

Disclaimer

This book is intended for readers age 18 and over. It contains mature situations and language that may be objectionable to some readers.

CONTENTS

JULIAN'S MATE

Prologue	3
Chapter 1	17
Chapter 2	32
Chapter 3	43
Chapter 4	58
Chapter 5	64
Chapter 6	71
Chapter 7	82
Chapter 8	86
Chapter 9	97
Chapter 10	107
Chapter 11	120
Chapter 12	134
Chapter 13	143
Also by Meg Ripley	151

JULIAN'S MATE

DADDY DRAGON GUARDIANS

PROLOGUE

Naomi rested her long, graceful neck on Julian's shoulder and admired the way the sun sparkled off his deep emerald scales, bringing out flecks of gold and purple. "They said there's nothing they can do," she said softly.

Julian's head moved swiftly, and he moved her off his shoulder so he could look into her eyes. "That can't be true. The mages know how to heal everything. Have they consulted with the witches as well?"

She was already tired. Naomi didn't know what this illness was, but it was slowly consuming her body. She could hardly sleep at night from the pain; during the day, she had so little energy, she was barely able to hunt for food. It was only because

Julian insisted on bringing her fresh meat that she hadn't starved to death. And then, of course, there had been the long climb to the top of Mount Taendru to visit the mages. It had taken the last of her spirit just to get there, and then they had given her the worst news she could have imagined.

"They have," Naomi affirmed. "But they've tried everything they know. Ervol even said he's seen this sort of thing before, but it's so rare, they don't have a name for it."

"There's got to be something." Julian was up now, pacing so quickly, he stirred up the thick red dirt under his clawed feet. They had come to their secret meeting place, a clearing in the woods on the far side of the mountains. It was where they had talked for hours into the night, made love, and made plans for their future together. But this time, there was no excitement or romance in their rendezvous.

"Not from them." She had known it would come to this, but still she didn't want to tell him. How could she get him to understand what a desperate position she was in? The life she was living wasn't one that was worth holding onto, and the risk just might be worth it. Still, it was impossible to explain.

Julian, sensing that she had more to say, stopped

pacing and turned a malachite eye to her. "What do you mean?"

Turning away to study the deep foliage that was such a contrast to the crimson rocky mountains that surrounded their settlement on Charok, Naomi searched for the right words. She only had one chance to do this right. If not, Julian might become angry with her or even try to stop her. She didn't want either one to happen, because she wanted to leave on good terms. "There is one thing that hasn't been tried yet, but it's not something the mages can do. It means that I'll have to go away."

"Okay." Julian's scaly lips tightened as he tried to remain patient. "You mean to gather a mineral in a distant mountain range or a plant that grows in a different set of woods?"

"No." She turned to look him in the eye now, knowing that he deserved it. He had been so good to her. "I'm going away permanently. I won't be back, ever."

"Naomi, you can't—"

"Don't try to stop me, Julian. You've got to promise me that you won't ask me any more about it or try to find out what I'm doing. And you can't follow me. You just can't." A tear leaked from the corner of her eye, though she thought she was all out of them.

"Whatever it is, just tell me! I can go with you. I can help in some way. But you can't just disappear and ask me never to wonder what happened!" His fists curled in the dirt, sending a red cloud into the air.

He was getting angry, and her instinct was to yell and rage right back at him. If she had been in good health, she might have done just that. Naomi had never been afraid to express her opinion around him, and it was one of the reasons that the two of them worked so well together. But she had no energy to argue, and there wasn't even time for it. She would have to leave soon. "If you love me, then you'll do what I'm asking," she pleaded, her words nearly carried away on the breeze they were so soft. "Please, Julian."

There was fire in his eyes, and he looked as though he was about to argue once again, but he took a deep breath instead. "When is this all supposed to happen?"

"As soon as possible."

"I don't even get to have one last night with you?"

A second tear followed the first one, and it

absorbed quickly in the warm ground. "No. I'm afraid not."

"And you're certain I can't come with you?" His voice was pleading now, desperate. "There's nothing that says I have to stay here. I won't be missed."

He would be, but Naomi knew she couldn't convince him of that. "Come with me back to the mountains, but beyond there, I have to continue alone." Even this was a compromise on her part. Naomi knew she could have told him to stay in that clearing for hours, and then there would be very little chance he would see where she was heading, but at least she would still be giving him something. Besides, she wasn't certain she could make it all the way back on her own.

They spoke very little as they journeyed. There was nothing much to say. Every now and then, Julian let his wing bump gently against hers, as though he was reminding her that he was still there. It would have been easier for them to fly, but that would have taken far more out of her than what she had.

When they stood once again on the rocky ledges of the mountains, she turned to him. "I have to go now. But I want you to know that I love you, Julian. I feel as though I've loved you my entire life, and I'm sorry that I won't get to spend the rest of it with you."

"I love you, too." He curled his neck around hers, letting his wings come forward to embrace both of their bodies. It wasn't the sort of thing they would have done a few weeks ago, before Naomi grew ill. The two of them had been determined to keep their relationship a secret as long as they could, unwilling to spoil it with the prying eyes and nosy wonderings of the other dragons. But it didn't matter now. Let them see, if anyone was around.

"I know you say you aren't coming back," Julian whispered, "but I'm going to wait for you anyway."

"No, don't do that," Naomi protested. "You deserve a chance to move on, to be happy."

He gave her a small smile, the barest upturn of one corner of his mouth. "I think we both know that can't happen. But thank you anyway."

Naomi turned and headed down the mountain path, veering to the left halfway down to travel north. Without looking back, she knew Julian was watching her. He stood on the top of the mountain, waiting to see if she would turn around and tell him she had changed her mind. But Naomi knew she couldn't change her mind. She would only die, and that wasn't going to help either one of them.

It was a long journey, and a hot one. Naomi had to stop and rest at shorter and shorter intervals, barely catching her breath before it was time to move on again. Her feet ached, and by the time she reached the bush of purple flowers that marked the hidden path, her wingtips were dragging on the ground. Her neck slung low, parallel to the ground, and she turned toward the woods once again.

The little hut was right where she had left it before, and Varhan swung open the door before he reached it. "Sit, sit!" he commanded as he came rushing out. "I can see that the journey has taken its toll."

"You could say that," Naomi whispered. She took no comfort from the shade of the trees or the padding of leaf litter underneath her. "I didn't think I would make it at all."

The wizard was at her side, his pale, fleshy fingers gently moving across her scales. "It's gotten quite bad, hasn't it?"

She tried to nod but only managed to slightly roll her head in the dead leaves on the ground.

"You're certain you understand how all of this works?" Varhan asked. "You have to be completely committed to the idea, or there's a chance that it may not work at all."

"I know what you said, that the energies are different in this other place. That I'll be healed simply by being there. What did you say it was called again?"

"Earth," Varhan replied. "It's an odd sort of place, but most of the creatures there are in human form, just like myself--or you, if you're so inclined. Do any of your people prefer to go around on two legs instead of four?"

"Not very often. Only when we have to, or if we go to the Great Court. You can fit a lot more dragons into a small space that way. But personally, I like my scales." Now that she thought about it, she might have had an easier time getting to the wizard's hut if she had shifted. But that took energy as well, and there was no telling if she could accomplish it anymore.

Varhan gave a soft laugh and ducked through the door of his hut. Naomi could hear him inside, rattling bottles and moving things around. "That's one of the reasons I've always found dragons to be so fascinating. In your own way, you can be even more stubborn than wizards."

"Is that why there's always someone arguing over land in the Great Basin?" Naomi wheezed. "Because everyone is too stubborn to compromise?"

The wizard shrugged as he emerged from his home, a roll of his shoulders under his tattered brown robe. He was by far the most humble wizard Naomi had ever met, and the only one who would condescend to talk to her. "That might be a large part of it, indeed. I hate to say it, but I wouldn't be surprised if our people ended up going to war. And over something so silly." He shook his head as he dipped a brush into a small clay jar and began painting a cool substance over her body, starting at the spine and working his way down. "The idea makes me sad. I think we have a lot to learn from each other."

"You're right." Naomi closed her eyes, enjoying the sensation of the salve. She didn't know what it was, but its cooling effect was glorious. It had seemed that her fire was constantly building up inside her since she'd fallen ill, but she couldn't seem to muster the desire to dispense of it. "And I don't even want to know what Julian or anyone else would think if they realized I had come to a wizard for help."

"Don't you worry about Julian. He'll be fine."

She swiveled her head to look at him, immediately setting her chin back on the ground after the effort. Still, she could see his round face and his dark hair. He was much younger than any of the other wizards she had seen. Maybe that was why he didn't carry the same biases as the others. "You know Julian?"

"I know a lot more than you might think." Varhan stretched up on his tiptoes to reach the long bones of her wings with his brush. "I've lived out here a long time, and I come out to talk to anyone who comes by. I've never been bold enough to march right into your town and make my presence known, but I've still managed to gather quite a bit of information."

Naomi was silent for a while as she watched him finish with the silvery substance. It made her blue scales, normally shiny, a matte grey color. "Do you really think this will work?"

Varhan took one last stroke of his paintbrush down her tail and returned to her head. He kneeled down in front of her, his grey eyes looking calmly into hers. "I do. I've studied long and hard. There are numerous factors at work here, but I think I can manipulate them in all the right ways to get you to Earth. But I need you to understand that this isn't as simple as transporting a being from one place to another. It pulls on the strings of the universe, changing and manipulating things in ways that even I wouldn't have imagined during my studies under Master Knexon. In other words, I'm changing your entire life as well as the lives of others."

"Am I putting anyone in danger? I'd rather die here than know I had blood on my claws."

"No, no." Varhan stood and went inside his hut once again, coming back out with a burlap sack. He began removing stones from it one by one, setting them in a large circle around the dragon. "I know most wizards aren't too concerned with who gets caught up in their spells, but I'm different. This whole thing is different." He paused, resting his fingers against his mouth for a moment as though unsure of how to proceed. "Naomi, I have studied the way the universe pulls at each of us as individuals, and I can tell you that this spell is going to have lasting effects. But they're going to be good ones. It's on Earth that you'll meet your true love."

Her heart rose in her chest, out of fear instead of hope. She had already met her mate, and he was there, on Charok. "But—"

"And your presence will ensure that three others meet the ones they're truly meant to be with, though they might not meet them otherwise. So take heart in knowing that not only are you saving yourself, but you're giving one of the greatest gifts to others as well."

This all sounded too good to be true, and Naomi didn't like the idea of not knowing for certain what was happening. "Varhan, I—"

"Hush," the wizard whispered. He turned an ear to the treetops, lifting his eyes to the sky for a moment. "We have to finish this quickly, or the opportunity will be missed. This application will protect you during the transition, but it only lasts so long." He placed the last of the stones around Naomi and began chanting. It was a language she didn't understand, but she knew this was no time to question him. Varhan moved around her, his hands waving quickly as he manipulated the very air around them. Soon enough, Naomi could see sparks flying from his fingers as he worked.

She gave one last thought to Julian. How she wished she could have told him what was happening, but she barely even understood it herself. This sickness, this disease that even the mages couldn't cure, was only going to resolve if she left the planet itself. And to make things even more shameful, it required the help of a wizard. The other dragons would never have let her go if they had known, and that was why she had not even told Julian the entire truth. If someone discovered what had happened, she didn't want him to be part of it.

Her scales tingled as the leaves on the forest floor began to swirl around her. The light from Varhan's fingers had now become streaks instead of sparks, and they joined the whirlwind. The ground trembled beneath her, but she no longer had the energy to be afraid as it dissipated. The wizard's chanting had either stopped or been lost in the sound of the wind, but either way, it didn't look like the spell needed him anymore. The dirt and leaves separated completely beneath Naomi, revealing a blackness deeper than anything she had seen before.

She felt one last tear leak from her eye as she fell through.

1

JULIAN AWOKE, PULLING IN A GASPING BREATH AS HE sat up in bed. He panted for a moment as he studied his surroundings, taking in the deep brown walls, hardwood floors, and framed abstract paintings on the walls. He knew he should recognize it all, but the dream world he had just come from stopped him at first. As Julian woke fully and his hands touched the soft blankets spread over him, he was once again hit with the hard reality of where he was. Earth.

He sank back onto the pillow with a sigh, closing his eyes to help retrieve whatever fragments of his dream he might still be able to recover before they were lost to the light of day. It wasn't the first time he had dreamed of Naomi, not since she had left him back on Charok and not since he and the other shifters had arrived on Earth almost a year ago. She visited him often, her cerulean scales and the delicate shift of her slitted eyes so clear in his mind that she could have been standing right in front of him. The visions were so realistic that at times he could reach out and touch her, feeling the thin skin that stretched between the bones of her wings.

And in those dreams, she was healthy. They always took place when she and Julian first met and fell in love, spending all of their time together in that hidden meadow in the woods where nobody else could see them. Julian knew that there was no real reason to keep their relationship a secret. Most of the dragons didn't have the same sort of odd sensibilities that Earthlings did about who their friends and family decided to be with. But it was fun, nonetheless, and they never had a chance to come out and declare their love publicly before she'd had to go.

So many times, Julian had wondered what had happened to her. Had she died on some craggy mountaintop on her way to this mysterious promise of health? Or had she been able to find what she needed and started a new life? It didn't really matter, since the War of Storms broke out only a few years later and killed every dragon on Charok. If she hadn't died from her illness, then she had surely died from the spell cast by the evil Tazarre.

Rolling over, Julian stretched and checked the time on the alarm clock. It wasn't even set to go off for another half an hour, but that was nothing unusual. He found that he had never been able to sleep as deeply in a soft bed as he had on the hard floor of a cave, and lately, the problem had only been getting worse. That was just as well, because he had plenty of studying to do before Kaylee awoke.

Slipping quietly past his daughter's bedroom and to the kitchen, Julian retrieved a mug from the cabinet and poured a large serving of coffee. While he hadn't found pleasure in everything that was involved in being a human on Earth, the black drink and the automated coffee pot were two things that he took great comfort in. He carried his cup to the library and sank down into a leather chair, putting his feet up on the matching ottoman.

Retrieving a Book of Shadows he had borrowed from Autumn, Julian stared at the cover for a moment, his mind slipping back to how he and his friends had gotten to Earth in the first place. Life had been good back on Charok, when they were free dragons living peacefully amongst the mountains. But no peace could last forever, and when the ogres started a war against the dragons over who had the right to use the Andrullian Lake, Julian wasn't certain it was worth fighting over. But the wizards, who had been disputing the land in the Great Basin, soon joined the fight. That was when he knew it was all over.

It was Tazarre, the leader of the wizards, who had come up with the spell that would kill all of dragonkind. He was confident enough to announce his plan for all species to hear, making even the ogres tremble before him. Julian had been studying a few spells himself, but it had never been anything more than a hobby. He didn't have anywhere close to enough knowledge to do anything about it. Even now, he could remember that day so clearly in his mind that the library disappeared around him, replaced by the woods on the far side of the mountains.

"*Varhan!*" *Julian trudged through the woods, not willing to risk flying. He would be seen instantly and taken down. From the horror stories he had been told, he would be tortured for several days before they finally killed him. Instead, he had opted for his bipedal form, feeling it was the safest bet.* "*Varhan, are you home?*"

To his relief, the little wizard came rushing out of his hut. His eyes were wild, his hair standing out from his head as though he had slept upside down. "Julian! What are you doing here, my friend? It's a death sentence for you, surely!"

"Yes, but you and I both know that I have death looming over my head, anyway. I've watched everyone around me die, slowly poisoned by the black magic that Tazarre has injected into every rock and blade of grass. There are so many carcasses on the mountainsides that we can't keep up with them." His eyes blurred, making the wizard little more than a pale, shadowy form. "I need your help, desperately."

"And what about the others?" Varhan looked behind Julian expectantly.

Julian's shoulders sagged a little, feeling shame for not trusting the wizard completely. "Yes, they're here with me, too. How did you know?" He had told his friends to stay behind until he knew whether or not it was safe for them to come. Julian had known Varhan for quite some time, visiting him at his little hut and learning everything he could about spells and magic. But he hadn't known if there would be other wizards around. What if they had discovered Varhan's sympathies for dragons and had set a trap?

"That's alright. I knew they would be. I've been

expecting you for a few days now. Tell them to come. We'll have to hurry."

Julian gave a whistle to the others. "What do you have planned?"

Varhan's lips pressed together, and he shifted his feet in the leaves. "Something I've been working on for a very long time. I'll be sending you someplace safe."

"But rumor has it that the entire planet is affected," Julian argued.

"I know. I know." Varhan stepped inside his hut, leaving the door open as he talked. "You won't be on Charok anymore."

"There's something you should know." By this time, Holden, Beau, and Xander had come up behind him, each carrying a heavy load. "We're not alone."

The wizard stepped back through the doorway, a small clay pot in his hand. He stirred the contents vigorously with a brush, but he stopped as soon as he saw what the other men carried. Stepping forward, Varhan laid a delicate finger on the silvery surface of the oblong item in Holden's arms. "Is that what I think it is?"

Holden gave the wizard a dirty look, but he held his head high as he answered. "The last four eggs of our queen, who now lies dead in her throne room. As far as we know, they're still viable."

Julian watched Varhan with a ball of despair in his throat. "Do you think you can help us? All of us?"

The man nodded slowly, and then more forcefully. "Yes. Yes, I can. This is perfect, actually. It's even better than I had anticipated. You'll all need to shift, though, and do it now. We don't have time to be shy about such things. If we don't get you out of here soon, there won't be anything I can do for you."

The dragons did as they were told, taking on the shapes they had been born with. It was usually a pleasurable experience, one that Julian looked forward to after he had spent some time as a man, but at the moment, he just wanted to get it over with. "Varhan," he said when he was finished, "you sound as though you knew this was coming."

"I did, but there's no time to really explain it. Just know that you're going where you're destined to be. Remember that, if nothing else. Now come here." The wizard reached up with the brush and began painting a sticky substance over Julian. "This will protect you in your journey. There should be enough for the eggs, as well."

EVEN NOW, Julian could still remember the way that bristly brush had felt against his scales. It had burned off completely by the time they had arrived on Earth, and so he could only assume it had done its job.

With a sigh and a shake of his head, Julian opened the Book of Shadows and found where he had left off the evening before. He had come no closer to finding a way to return to Charok, no matter how many books he read. Xander had a library filled with books about humans and life on Earth, but Julian's collection consisted almost purely of books about spells, hexes, voodoo, and otherworldly experiences. It might take forever, but he still held out hope they could return to Charok with their children and that perhaps some of the dragons there would have been spared.

Kaylee awoke half an hour later when Julian was deep into a section about protection spells. "Da-deeee!" she called from her room.

Julian eagerly set the book down and hopped to his feet, trotting down the hall to retrieve his baby girl. She might not have been his by blood, but bringing her across the universe in the form of an egg was enough of a bond for him. With her olive tones and brilliant green eyes, she looked every bit as though he had fathered her.

"Good morning, sweet thing," he cooed as he

lifted her out of her crib and hugged her. "Did you have any good dreams?"

She grinned at him and wrapped her arms around his neck. "Doughnuts?" she asked.

Julian had to laugh. He'd made the mistake of letting her experience the sweet breakfast treat two weeks ago, and she hadn't stopped talking about them since. "No, I think we'll go with scrambled eggs and some toast, instead. Then we'll go see your Uncle Holden for a little bit."

"Otay!"

An hour later, they pulled up in front of the massive house Holden had chosen as they each settled into their new life on Earth. On the outskirts of town, it was the sort of place that was apparently very impressive to most humans. Though he couldn't be certain, Julian imagined Holden had picked it out because the roofline reminded him of the mountains back on Charok.

"You're just in time," Holden said as he flung open the front door. "Leah has just left for work, and Finn has already been asking what we're going to do today. I'm sure he'd love to play with Kaylee for a bit."

"I thought about taking her to the park, but it looks like it's going to rain." Julian stepped into the foyer and set down his diaper bag. "Besides, I wanted to talk to you, and it isn't the sort of thing I would want the other parents at the park to hear."

"Oh?" Holden led the way down the hall to Finn's bedroom, where his little boy was stacking up wooden blocks until they were as tall as he was. He clapped and grinned when he saw his cousin.

Julian set Kaylee down, watching with satisfaction as she crawled over to play. He'd been putting off this conversation for a while, content to wait things out as long as he could, but there wasn't much choice but to bring it all out in the open now. "Do you remember, when Varhan was sending us here, that he said we were going where we were destined to be?"

"Of course, I do." Holden leaned against the doorway and folded his arms in front of his wide chest. "I have to admit I wasn't very certain about him when you first said there was a wizard who might help us. After all, I had seen what Tazarre and the others had done. But there was something about the way Varhan spoke, like he knew far more than we did. It's what let me know we were doing the right thing."

Looking down at Kaylee, who had picked up a block and was turning it over to examine each side of it, he nodded. "And I think in many ways, we did. We saved the children from a doomed fate."

Holden scratched his chin. "I have to admit that I was worried at first. If we were meant to be here, then in my mind, that implied we would find our mates here as well. But I knew we had to, for the children's sake, and I can see now that Varhan really was right. Xander, Beau, and myself are all taken care of. Now I just have to find a way to get you out of the house."

"That's exactly what I wanted to talk to you about. I've made a few efforts, as you know, hoping that you were right. But there's more to the equation that you don't know, and I don't think I will find my mate here." He should have brought it up a long time ago, but it never seemed like the right time.

"What are you talking about?"

With a sigh, Julian tried to make as short of a story as possible about Naomi. "I already met my mate, back on Charok."

Holden raised an eyebrow. "You never told me that."

"We didn't tell anyone. We didn't want the pressure of going through formal ceremonies, and it was exciting to have our little trysts. But she got sick and she left in search of some cure she wouldn't tell me about. She's dead now, just like all the others." He thought it would make him feel better to tell Holden, but the weight of the telling was heavy on his shoulders like iron. Somehow it didn't make things any better to admit out loud that he would never see her again.

His friend stood for a long time, his lips slightly pursed as he studied the floor. "I see," he finally said.

"I thought you should know because you've always been the one encouraging us and giving us hope of having a real family here on Earth. I have Kaylee, and I have you guys. Now I have Summer, Autumn, and Leah as well. But it's never going to be more than that." He had taken comfort in knowing that he wasn't the only dragon on Earth. Having the children around made a difference, and so did knowing that his friends were happy with their mates. Some days that was enough, and some days it wasn't. Right then, after yet another vivid dream about Naomi, it wasn't.

Holden's thick hand clapped him on the shoulder. "You don't know that."

Julian snapped his eyes up. "Did you not hear what I just told you? I already found my fated mate. I felt the fire burning inside me anytime we were apart. I even tried to take on a human form around her, just to prove to myself that I couldn't keep it for more than a few minutes before I had to shift back. I had her, and now she's gone." Frustration and anger built up in his chest all over again, and he wished he could shift right at that moment just to vent it all out in a massive ball of flame.

"I heard you," Holden assured him calmly. He never got bent out of shape, not unless someone was threatening his woman or his child. "But I'm not entirely convinced."

"Are you seriously going to tell me I don't know how to tell when I've found the one? I might have been a bit younger when it happened, but I wasn't stupid. It's a fairly unmistakable feeling." He wouldn't fight Holden, not over something so stupid, but the urge was definitely there.

Holden gave a light laugh. "I'm not saying that at all. Calm down. I was just thinking about the fact that none of us were very confident we would find our mates, but three out of the four of us have. Maybe your first love is gone, and I hate the thought of that, but it doesn't mean that you're completely out of luck."

"I think you've been on Earth too long and you've forgotten that we're not actually human." Julian knew perfectly well that humans all *thought* they had one special person out there waiting for them, but in reality, they fell in love over and over again.

"Just listen, okay? I've thought about this a lot, even though I know that Leah is the one person I'm supposed to be with. But we're not talking about dragons being with dragons. We're talking about dragons being with humans, and maybe that's different. Maybe we're not restricted to just one person. Maybe there's more than one who could make us happy. It's impossible to say, and I hoped that none of us would ever need to find out, but I guess you'll be our experiment."

"Gee, thanks." Julian was pretty sure Holden had been spending too much time with Xander, making anthropological theories that they had no real way of proving. "I feel so honored."

"I just don't want to see you go through your life with no one at your side. I know it's made a big difference for me, and I'd like to think that it will for you, too. I know you've got to be heartbroken, but don't let that affect the rest of your life. Consider that it will affect Kaylee, too."

"Oh, I have." Julian had weighed the consequences either way. It would be good for his daughter to have a mother in her life. She loved the other women, but it would be different if she had someone to call her own. But if Julian didn't pick the right woman—something that could easily happen since he wouldn't feel the same sort of wild emotions that happened when a dragon met his true love—it could also cause great devastation for Kaylee. What if they didn't get along and the woman he chose left? Then his daughter would be worse off than she had been in the first place. He did his best to communicate these concerns to Holden.

"Don't give up just yet," he advised. "I know I haven't given up on you."

2

Autumn's house was quiet, but it was clear to the three women who sat on the floor around a candle that they weren't completely alone. They had cast their circle and called to the spirit guides, hoping to make a good connection with Naomi.

Feeling a distinct sensation of being watched, Autumn slowly opened her eyes. The image of the blue dragon that hovered in the air above the flame was faint this time. In fact, she could see Leah's solemn face right though it. But the dragon was there, nonetheless.

"Naomi! We've been trying so hard to reach you. We've had several seances lately with no success. I was beginning to worry about whether or not you were still there." She hadn't yet figured out exactly where 'there' was, but the spirit realm in which their friend now existed seemed to be one with a thick veil around it.

"I'm here," Naomi said faintly, "but it takes a lot of energy to keep the door between the worlds open. And I'm not always alone."

"Are you in danger?" Leah asked, her blue eyes desperate.

The dragon's head rolled on her long neck. "Yes and no."

"What does that mean?" Summer's long blonde hair fell forward over her shoulders as she leaned toward the apparition. "Please, Naomi. We've been so worried about you."

Naomi watched them, turning slowly to look at them each in turn. "I'll be fine."

And in an instant, she was gone.

Autumn, feeling the weight and pressure of their circle suddenly broken, lay back on the floor and spread her arms wide. "Do you think we'll ever get to talk to her for more than a few minutes? I thought I had a decent technique down, but I'm starting to question myself."

"Don't go getting yourself a 9-to-5 job just yet," Leah advised, rubbing her hands down her face. "It's exhausting for all of us. I would have hoped that knowing her as we did would make this easier. Maybe it has something to do with the fact that she's in dragon form all the time in the spirit realm."

"At least she seems to be." Autumn had been thinking about this a lot ever since they had started their seances to try to reach Naomi. "I swear it's like she isn't either one at first, not until we call to her. It makes me wonder if there's some other shape she can take, or if we're just interpreting her as being a dragon because that's how our minds understand her."

"That's an interesting proposition." Summer, Autumn's twin, bent over her stretched legs like a ballet dancer warming up for a show. "We only saw her transition into dragon form, what, once?"

Autumn nodded. "She was always so private about it." The three of them had met Naomi back in college, back when they were still trying to figure out who they were and where they belonged in society. Leah was a psychic, and the twins were witches, which made it difficult to get along with their peers sometimes. Naomi had been a perfect addition to the group.

"For a long time, I wondered if she was telling us the truth about being a dragon," Summer admitted. "Not that I ever thought she was doing it to be dishonest, but like that was just her excuse for not being the same as everyone else. Naomi was so quiet and reserved, like she was uncomfortable being on Earth, even."

"And I guess we all understand that a lot more now." Autumn had talked with her boyfriend about this quite a bit since they'd gotten together a few months ago. He, like the others, was a dragon shifter from Charok. Summer had paired up with Xander, and Leah had been the first one of them to discover that there were still dragons on Earth when she started dating Holden.

"Isn't it ironic," Leah mused, "that a dragon had been a part of our lives for several years, and then we all ended up with dragons? Naomi had said she was the only one, and I guess she would have been at that time since Holden and the others weren't here yet. But I had never considered the possibility that more of them might come. Or that they might be so hot." She grinned.

Autumn had to agree. "I just wish we could talk to her longer about where she is. I'd love to find a way to get her back. If she had come across the universe once already, then it doesn't seem so unlikely that we might be able to free her from the spirit realm as well."

The three women were silent for a moment, remembering, until Summer spoke. "I remember so clearly the day she died," she said quietly, her wide eyes still trained on the candle flame even though they all knew the séance was over. "At that point, we knew for certain that she was a dragon, and it seemed so unreal that she could die from something like a car accident. That was the part that hit me the most, that even though none of us are just normal humans, we're still very mortal."

Autumn closed her eyes and was instantly transported to the hospital. She'd received a phone call, but that part had been blotted from her memory. Instead, what she recalled most was bursting into the emergency room, the smell of antiseptic whacking her in the face and trying to shove her back outside into the fresh air where she belonged. But she surged forward instead, trying to keep her voice steady as she asked the woman at the desk about her friend.

The surgeons were busy working on her, but even that hadn't given Autumn hope. What was the anatomy and physiology of a dragon shifter like? Would the normal procedures and medications even work on her? Or would they be able to save her, only to have the government swoop in and keep her for experiments once they realized she was different?

In the end, none of that had mattered. Naomi had died on the table, and none of the doctors acted as though anything strange had happened.

"She was a good friend," Autumn said with a sigh. "I feel like I'm being a bad one since I can't bring her back."

"Stop that." Leah stood and crossed the room to a low table, pouring herself a glass of wine. "I want Naomi back just as much as you do, but I don't think most people expect to be brought back from the dead. We're doing what we can, and it's not like we've given up yet."

But the truth was that Autumn had considered it. She'd tried every spell she could think of, and nothing had worked. There was very little in her spell books that she hadn't thoroughly examined and tested. Even if she did somehow manage to open a portal between their two worlds and drag Naomi back, what about her physical body? There were so many complications, and it didn't give her much hope for the future.

"The truth is stranger than fiction." Summer had muttered the words so quietly, Autumn wasn't sure she had heard her correctly.

"What?"

Summer rose and followed Leah's example, pouring herself a generous glass of Merlot before returning to her cushion on the floor. The candlelight danced in her golden hair as she took a slow sip and then tipped her head back. "I've been watching a lot of movies lately. It's not the kind of thing I normally like to do, and I'd be fine with not even owning a TV, but Xander really likes them. He says they tell him a lot about what it means to be human, because people take all the things they want from life and make them into movies."

"Are you sure that's your first glass?" Autumn challenged. "I thought we were talking about Naomi."

Her sister gave her a sassy look. "It is, and we are. Just be patient for a minute. Xander's big thing right now is scary movies. We have to wait until Nora is in bed, because we don't want to scare her, and then we cuddle up on the couch. A lot of them are ones that I saw as a kid, but I notice so much more about them now than I ever did. And you should hear some of the questions Xander asks me! If he watched nothing but horror movies, he would think humans were complete idiots."

"The point, Summer?" Autumn knew she

shouldn't be impatient with her, but she also knew that she had done more research on this than anyone else in the group had. If she didn't know how to bring Naomi back, then she doubted anyone else would. And some dumb movie wasn't going to help them, since they were living in the real world.

"The point is that I've seen numerous movies where someone gets sucked into a ghost world of some sort, and then they *send someone in* to retrieve them. It's not about casting the right spell or anything, it's more of a physical solution." Her face was alight as she explained, as though she had just come up with a Nobel Prize-worthy theory.

"It's a friggin' movie, Summer, not real life. The people who write those movies have no idea what magic is really like." And it was for that exact reason Autumn didn't usually bother watching movies like that. She didn't mind a romantic comedy or even a drama, but it annoyed her to no end when people pretended to know something about magic.

Her sister sighed. "I know they don't. Or at least, as far as we know they don't. But there might be some logic to the scenario."

"Right now, the only thing we're able to do is open up a window for us to look through and talk to

Naomi. That's it. There's nothing like a room for a person," Autumn argued.

"It's an interesting theory, though," Leah volunteered. "And it might not be exactly what we're looking for, but I think it's worth exploring. I was hoping we could get at least enough of a connection that I could establish a psychic link with her. Maybe that way, I could get a good understanding of exactly what's going on with her. But so far, that hasn't worked. We've got to keep our minds open to any option."

"Yeah, I guess you're right." Autumn followed suit with the others and poured her own drink. It was a good wine, one that Leah had picked up on the way over. She never went cheap on things now that her psychic business and her books were doing so well. "I'm just so frustrated because I've spent a lot of time on this. I consider it my goal in life at this point, and I haven't made any progress."

"It's a process of elimination, at least," Summer offered. "I wonder if maybe the guys can help us."

This was something that had occurred to Autumn already, especially when Julian had asked to borrow some spell books from her. "I wish I could say that they can, but I don't think it's possible. Julian likes to study spell books, and even did when he still lived on Charok. But it's more of a scholarly knowledge than applied. Even *he* doesn't know much about the spell that brought them to Earth. It happened so quickly, and he's spent months trying to figure out how to replicate it, but to no avail."

"Surely that's different from what we're talking about," Leah mused. "In some way, at least. It's probably still worth talking to him about it."

"I'll do that next time I see him."

When the other women had gone home and it was time for Autumn to go back to the place she shared with Beau, she hesitated. This house was now completely dedicated to her spiritual needs. She had Beau and Elliot at her new home, and she was able to dedicate this space to meditation, storing herbs, and working new spells. She and the other women had a private, sacred place for seances and spellwork. It was a wonderful sort of freedom, and Beau never demanded that she be home early or stop what she was doing simply because he wanted to be with her. He respected that she needed her privacy and her alone time, especially when it came to focusing in on what she truly was: a witch. But all the space and time and materials in the world didn't seem to be enough to bring Naomi back.

She couldn't help but feel that there was something she was missing, something she should have seen a long time ago. She reached out to Naomi in her mind, knowing that she couldn't possibly even say hello without the help of the others, but determined to do it anyway. There was nothing there for her. With a sigh, Autumn picked the cushions up off the floor, grabbed her purse and locked the door on the way out.

3

A week later, Autumn had managed to shrug off the heavy weight of her mostly unsuccessful séance. It would be another month before they would try again, since they would only drain themselves of all their energy if they attempted contact too often. Instead, Leah was across the street doing psychic readings and Autumn and Summer were back at work at The Enchanted Elm.

Running a new age store in a small town was often a challenge, but it was one that Autumn enjoyed. She had dealt with other business owners who didn't appreciate a couple of witches running a shop next door, and she had handled the religious fanatics who didn't accept the Keller sisters as part of the community. That was in addition to the ordinary challenge of finding just the right profit margin to keep the money coming in without driving the customers away. And with her business degree, that was just the sort of thing Autumn was good at.

Taking care of her customers and running a successful business was just what she was thinking about when the bell over the front door rang. Autumn was bent over the counter, deciding whether or not to buy a sponsorship in the program for the high school spring play. She glanced up at the man, ready with her usual spiel of offering to help if he needed anything, but she could tell by the confused look on his face that he was going to need assistance right away.

"Good morning. What can I help you find?"

The man was young, probably in his early twenties, and his eyes were the same cool grey as the clouds that had been hanging over the town all morning, threatening with a rain shower, but never actually coming through on it. He glanced at Autumn as he approached the counter, but quickly averted his eyes to the floor as he rubbed his face.

"Well, um, I don't know if you'll have what I'm looking for..."

"Even if I don't, I can probably find it for you. We do special orders all the time." Usually, customers at

The Enchanted Elm knew little enough about magic that they were able to walk in and buy whatever caught their eye. But there were still a few folks who wanted a specific scent of incense or candle or who felt their cousin in Ohio would prefer a teal dreamcatcher instead of a purple one. Sometimes, Autumn or Summer would need to order a particular crystal they knew was needed to heal a client.

"Well, it's sort of strange. I don't think it has anything to do with Wicca." He had reached the counter now, and he shifted his weight from foot to foot.

"That doesn't matter," Autumn assured him, growing more curious by the moment as to just what this man was searching for. "We supply all sorts of belief systems with no discrimination."

He nodded, finally looking up at her again. "Okay, here's the thing. I saw a show recently about shamanism, and I thought it might really help me. I spent several years on drugs, and I've been trying to get my life back together. I'm clean, I've got a job, and I've even got a girlfriend, but I just feel like there's a part of me missing. The guy on TV was talking about soul retrieval, and that it's a way to find the pieces of yourself that you don't have access to. Like maybe I could use a shamanic ritual to gain access to the parts of my brain that I cut off with all the drugs, you know?" He talked faster and faster as he went on, and a few beads of sweat popped out on his forehead. "I'm sorry. I don't know why I'm telling you all this."

But Autumn understood exactly why, even if he didn't. "Because you want to be healed, and it's a scary process that you can't always do alone. I understand. I've heard of soul retrieval, though I admit I don't have any experience with it. What particular supplies do you need?"

"A drum, apparently. Or at least, that's one way to get started. The sound of the drum beating puts you in a sort of trance, where you can access other parts of yourself or the world or something. I don't understand all of it yet."

"Let me see." Autumn began looking through their inventory to see if they had anything that would work. "Are you having someone beat the drum for you, or are you doing it yourself?"

"My therapist says he'll do it with me. It's new to both of us, but he was really excited when I brought the idea to him. He says he has lots of patients who are going through the same stuff I am, so if this is successful, he might even start doing it on a regular basis."

Autumn desperately wanted to ask him the name of his therapist and if he was there in town. Any time she found someone who was open-minded like that, she liked to take note. "That's wonderful. It's always good to have someone navigating for you when you're on a spiritual journey. I don't have anything in stock at the moment that will be quite right for you, but I can order something. Here." She turned the screen around to show him. "My supplier has these drum sets in stock, and if you like one of them, I can have it here within a couple of days."

His eyes widened at he bent to look at the screen. "Yeah! That's just like what the guy on TV was using. I'll take one of the cheaper sets. I don't want to spend a lot of money until I know if it works or not."

"Completely understandable." Autumn rang up the transaction and put in the order, requesting a couple of extra sets to put in the shop's inventory as well. If this guy wanted drums, then someone else might, too. She gave him a copy of the receipt. "I'll give you a call as soon as it comes in. If you don't mind sharing, I'd love to know how this goes for you. Feel free to stop in and tell me about it."

He smiled, looking more positive than he had since he'd first walked in. "Thanks. I'll do that."

When he had left and the store was quiet once

again, Autumn turned back to the form for the school play. She knew that buying a small place in the back of the program wouldn't actually bring in any new business, but she liked the idea of supporting the drama club and being a part of the community. But even as she wrote out a check, she found that she wasn't all that interested in advertising and marketing anymore.

Her mind returned again and again to the young man's request for shamanic drums. Maybe it was time to expand her own horizons. She clicked open her browser and began her research.

"Look, I know it's different than everything we've done before, but that's exactly why I want to try it." Autumn had gathered her friends in her house, feeling hopeful and tentative. The sun shone through the big windows on the back of the house as they shared a Saturday morning brunch and mimosas. She'd done weeks' worth of research without saying anything, wanting to make sure she had all the information before she brought it to the others.

"It *is* different," Summer acknowledged, a small

smile playing on her lips, "but only in a few ways. It seems more like a cousin of what we do on a regular basis. We'll still call in the directions and cast a circle." She sat in the breakfast nook with her knees pulled up to her chest.

Autumn herself was dressed and ready for the day in a pale lavender top and khakis. She considered it her weekend casual look, even though it was far more formal than what either of the other women were wearing. "Yes, but someone will need to go into a trance instead of casting a spell. I know I dismissed the idea you had about going in to retrieve Naomi like they do in the movies, but I can see now that there is some legitimate theory behind it. We're not physically tying a rope around your waist and shoving you through a portal, but it's sort of the psychic equivalent." As she was discovering more and more about shamanic rituals, Autumn had realized that the scenes her sister had described were simply fun, cinematic ways of showing something that was done on a fairly regular basis in certain communities.

"And what about her physical body?" Leah asked. She stood from the table and stepped to the breakfast bar to mix herself another mimosa. "We know that our world doesn't support spirits on their own for very long."

"I've thought about that, too. I had to do a lot of digging, but I found a spell that we can use in conjunction with the ritual. It should create a new body for her, and Naomi's spirit will still dictate what it looks like. It calls for very basic ingredients, since everything in the universe is made of the same stuff anyway." She pulled a piece of paper out of a folder and set it in the middle of the table. "Basically dirt, plants, and stones. The spell wouldn't be anything on its own, but if we're successful in bringing Naomi back, then I think it will work."

"And I suppose you plan on being the one who goes into the trance?" Summer asked.

"I thought I would be a good candidate," Autumn affirmed. "I'm the one who's been doing the studying, so it makes sense."

"That's only because you left us out of it up until this point." Summer's words were pointed, but her look was gentle. "But that's alright. I'm down for this whenever you're ready."

"Same here," Leah said with a smile. "I'll even beat the drums for you."

THEIR ENTHUSIASM WOULDN'T HOLD them long, and as soon as the moon was right, the women were upstairs in Autumn's house, standing in a circle in the center of the room. The windows, one facing each direction, were open all the way to let in the fresh spring air and the sound of the gentle rain that had begun falling just as the sun went down.

They had called in the directions and cast their circle, and Autumn felt the familiar tingle of a safe ceremony fall on her shoulders. There was no better feeling than knowing she was about to explore something new and exciting in the spirit realm. Her heart leaped in her throat as she turned to face the other women, excited for this to begin.

"Every ritual is different, depending on who is performing it and what the intentions are. For now, we'll rely on the drum beats to induce the trance. If I can bring Naomi back, then Summer, I'll need you to perform the spell for her body."

Her sister nodded, the excitement equal in her eyes. She adjusted her fingers on the hand carved drumsticks she held. "Sounds good."

Summer and Leah began beating. They had been practicing together for the last couple of days, making sure that they could create a rhythm that was easy to keep going for long periods of time and worked on being in sync with each other. It was a simple set of four beats, louder at the beginning and growing slightly softer toward the end.

Autumn tipped her head back and closed her eyes, watching the way the candle threw light and shadow at her eyelids. She began her normal mediation routine, consciously relaxing each part of her body beginning at the top of her head and working her way slowly down to her toes. There was no concern about keeping track of time or worrying about how long this entire ritual might take. It could last all night, and they would continue it on into the next day if they had to. There were numerous accounts of shamanic rituals that lasted for hours or even days, with the resulting exhaustion only enhancing the results.

With her body loose and feeling light, Autumn turned her focus to her breathing. She concentrated on filling every corner of her lungs with air, inflating them to their fullest potential before she expelled every atom.

Just as she was about to focus on a mantra, Autumn heard an odd sound to her left. She dismissed it and brought her mind back to her breath, not wanting to lose the progress she had already made. It was going to be a long and perhaps difficult journey to get into a trance and open up the window between the realms in order to fetch Naomi.

But the sound came again, and she couldn't help but open her eyes. The candle was the only source of light in the room, but it was too bright. Autumn squinted, thinking it was just because she had been closing her eyes for so long, but she soon realized that it was burning brighter and hotter than it normally did.

Summer moaned again, that same noise that had brought Autumn out of her meditative state in the first place. Her head was tipped back on her shoulders so that she faced the ceiling, but her eyes were rolled so far back in her head that only the whites were visible. It was as though she was bending her body backwards to look behind herself. Despite this, her hands kept moving rhythmically on the drums.

Concern grew in Autumn's mind, and as she looked across the circle to Leah, she saw that same worry reflected in her eyes. This wasn't the plan. But what if Summer had already achieved the trance? It might not be safe to pull her out of it. There was no good or clear choice but to continue.

Autumn closed her eyes and focused on her breathing once again, but instead of looking to achieve the trance state herself, she channeled all her energy to her sister. She could feel it flowing through her veins now, like bright blue streaks of lightning, and she pushed every bit of it to Summer.

It was enough. Her sister's moans turned to odd gurgling noises, and her head began to sway so that her hair danced across the floor behind her. Still, her hands kept the rhythm, and for the first time since they were kids, Autumn felt a genuine fear of what they were doing. She was confident in her practice and in her knowledge, but they were stepping into new territory. It was one thing to put herself at risk, but it was something completely different to do that to her sister.

Don't stop it. Autumn heard the voice clear as a bell in her head, and she snapped her eyes across the circle to meet Leah's.

Autumn herself wasn't a psychic, and it had been a long time since the three of them had attempted to communicate telepathically, but she did her best. *Is she alright?*

I can't see anything, but she's okay.

The message was cryptic to Autumn at first, but she took this to mean that although Leah couldn't see into Summer's mind and interpret exactly what was happening, she didn't detect any danger. That would have to be good enough for the moment. It was killing her not to know all the details, but she didn't seem to have a choice. The drums had called to Summer.

Summer's noises grew more intense and more frequent now, and they quickly built up to a scream that deafened Autumn's ears. She was writhing now, her shoulders moving at odd angles and her spine undulating like a piece of grass in the breeze.

Autumn no longer bothered with closing her eyes. She needed to know what was happening, and she spoke aloud to Leah this time. "What's going on?"

"I don't know, exactly." There were tears in Leah's eyes. "I've tried to see through her eyes, but it's not working. It might if I touch her, but I don't want to risk it. Wherever she's at, though, I don't think she's here." Leah reached out with tentative fingers, spreading them out near Summer but keeping just a few inches of space. "I'm pretty sure she's not alone."

With a spike of adrenaline pushing at her heart, Autumn couldn't take her eyes off of Summer. "Does that mean she has Naomi?" Her fingers itched to begin the next spell. This was going to take a lot out of all of them by the time it was over, but for the moment, she had more energy than she knew what to do with. Not for the first time, she wished she had more of a coven to help her.

"I don't know," Leah replied honestly. "We'll have to wait and see."

Summer's spasms carried on for several more minutes until the candle's light burned so brightly that the pillar of wax exploded. Droplets of hot wax cascaded through the room, but somehow, the flame was still alight. Just above it, the air congealed and swirled, as though Autumn was looking at the room through a puddle. The swirling intensified, growing faster until a rupture formed in the center. A brilliant blue dragon writhed inside it, mirroring Summer.

Acting quickly, Autumn checked that the dish of fresh earth was placed directly next to the candle. Some wax had gotten in it, but there was nothing to be done about that now. She dug her hands down into the dirt as she chanted the words she had committed to memory, asking her spirit guides to form a new vessel for her friend. "Take this earth, as it is the mother of all of us, and build a new body that it might contain a spirit. Take these stones, as they are the bones of all of us, and create new bones that might hold her upright. Take these plants, as they are the nourishment of all of us, and nourish her new home."

The vision of the blue dragon writhed and coiled around itself. It was small, as though they were seeing it from a distance, but Autumn knew it could only be Naomi. "Just keep doing what you're doing, Summer," she whispered. "I'll have it all ready for you when you get back." The energy that she had been giving to her sister she now pushed down into the bowl.

As the vortex opened wider, the dirt, stones, and plants in the bowl rose up into the air, the particles scattering out into a wide sphere. Naomi's form emerged into the room, limp and lifeless as though she were floating on an invisible sea. Her body was brilliantly blue, the same color as Autumn's energy, but where a speck of dirt stuck to her, she became a deeper shade. More and more of the pieces flew to her, clinging to her for a moment before sinking in and leaving a deep cerulean shadow in their wake until she looked like she was freckled with the depths of the ocean. Soon enough, she was entirely the color of lapis lazuli.

In one swift moment, the flame went out. Naomi fell to the floor with a hard thud, and the vortex slammed shut.

4

JULIAN STOOD AT THE BACK OF THE BIG ROOM IN THE library, willing his mind to stay focused on the story. It was just some children's book about a young elephant who didn't feel that he fit in his own skin. It probably wasn't all that poignant to most of the kids who sat and looked at the pictures as the old woman read it to them, though he knew it could be a good lesson for Kaylee. She had two different skins to learn to love, after all.

But his mind had been covered by a cloud all day, and as he thought about it, even last night. He hadn't been able to get to sleep for several hours. Every time he closed his eyes, he could think of nothing but Charok and the numerous events that had happened there. None of the memories that came to mind were good ones. He was haunted by visions of Naomi, ill and dragging herself across the mountains, or the dead bodies of all his comrades as they lay in the red dirt. In the morning, after several cups of coffee, he'd thought he was finally ready to start his day. He'd chased the heavy feeling from his eyelids and he was determined to make sure Kaylee enjoyed their day together. But even something as simple as taking his daughter to story time at the library seemed difficult, and he felt restless as he waited for the book to be over.

"Which one is yours?" whispered a voice next to him.

"Hmm?" Julian turned to see a young woman smiling up at him. She had blonde hair that bounced around her shoulders and big brown eyes. She looked like she was dressed to go to the bar instead of the library. "Oh, the one in the front with the pink shirt." He pointed at Kaylee, where she sat raptly watching the storyteller.

"She's an absolute doll!" The woman had deep dimples when she smiled. "Mine is over there in the purple. Maybe we should get them together to play sometime, and you and I can have coffee."

There was nothing wrong with her suggestion. After his discussion with Holden, he had started to think that perhaps his friend was right. Just because he had known Naomi back on Charok didn't mean that he couldn't find someone to be with here. But thinking it was a possibility was an entirely different thing than acting on it. This woman next to him was attractive, and it was clear that she knew what life with kids was like. She might be a perfectly good candidate for any other guy, but the idea made his skin itch so badly, he wanted to scratch it off. "Um, I've got a lot going on right now. I don't think I'll have the time."

She pouted, shrugged, and turned her attention back to the story.

Julian tried to do the same, but his mind wouldn't shut off. He could see Naomi on the inside of his eyelids every time he blinked, and his entire body seemed to vibrate with the need to find her. She was gone. She was dead. No matter how hard he looked, he would never see her again. But his blood was boiling in his veins as though she were right in the next room, waiting for him to come to her.

Unable to stand it any longer, he carefully picked his way through the crowd of children on the floor and scooped Kaylee into his arms.

"Story!" she wailed.

"Sshh. Let's not ruin it for everyone else." Julian

trotted out of the library as quickly as possible, avoiding the curious stares of the other parents. He'd already made a scene, and it was only going to get worse. Kaylee loved story time. He tried to explain as he trotted across the damp parking lot and opened the car door. "I'm sorry, sweetie. I really am. But I've got an emergency."

She looked up at him with damp eyes as he buckled her in. "Story?" One large tear clung to her eyelashes.

It broke his heart, but he knew as a father that there were going to be many more of those tears in the future. He got behind the wheel. "I'm sorry. We'll come again next week, and maybe we can check out the book the librarian was reading. I know you don't understand right now, but if everything works out, then you will someday."

Julian fired up the engine and dialed Holden before he was even out of the lot. "Are you available to watch Kaylee today?" he asked without preamble.

"Sure," the deep voice replied. "But are you okay? You sound like you're upset."

Julian tightened his jaw, knowing there was no good way to explain. "Yeah, I'm okay. Essentially. I've just got something I've got to take care of."

"Sounds to me like you've got a woman. I don't

think I've heard that much urgency in your voice since we arrived on Earth," he laughed.

Grateful that he had Holden on his headset so Kaylee couldn't hear, Julian was tempted to argue. Naomi wasn't just a woman. She was far more than that. She was also *dead.* But he could practically hear her calling to him, sending her need for him out through the universe. He didn't know what he would need to do to find her, but he would do whatever it took. "Something like that."

"Well, bring the kiddo on over and take your time. Leah was out late last night, so Finn and I were just going to do some baking while she slept."

Kaylee's tears dried as soon as she realized she was going to get to play with her cousin. Julian dropped her off as quickly as he could, ready to focus on these strange urges that were taking over his body and figure out just what the hell he was going to do about them.

But Holden stopped him on the front steps. "Julian, whatever is going on, just know that we've all been through it."

Julian knew what he meant. There was a certain rage that took over a male dragon when he found his mate, and it made life very difficult for a little while. "I know. I'm not sure if this is that or something else.

I'll keep you posted. And thanks." He took off, knowing his daughter was in good hands.

Back behind the wheel of his car, Julian started driving. He didn't really know where he was going, and he paid no attention to speed limits. Allowing his body to take over and trying not to think about it too much, he wound his way back into town and down side streets. He was getting closer, and when his bones shook against one another, he stomped the brake. Julian looked up.

He had seen this house before. Hell, he'd even been inside it for a New Year's Eve party. It was Autumn's house, but her car wasn't in the driveway as he pulled up. "This is weird," Julian muttered to himself. He knew Autumn because of Beau, and he had borrowed a few books from her, but he couldn't say that they had been particularly close. He got out and looked up at the front of the place, wondering what the hell was going on. There was no good reason for him to be at her house. And he knew there was really no good reason for what he was about to do. But he tucked his shoulder and prepared to break down the front door.

5

Naomi could see the exhaustion on their faces. "You should go and rest. I know you're all as tired as I am, at least." She had slipped back into her human form as soon as she realized she was back on Earth, glad to finally shed the mantle of her dragon physique. Most shifters preferred to be their scaled selves, but for the moment, it seemed easier to be a human. That form didn't require as much energy to sustain.

"I'm worried about leaving you," Autumn said as she leaned over the bed. "You've been away for so long, and we've never done these spells before." She had explained briefly what they had done to get her back to Earth, talking of drums and shamans and other things Naomi didn't have the presence of mind to even try to understand.

"The Otherworld," Naomi whispered. It was what she had come to call the place where she had gone after she died. Humans had concepts of heaven and hell and places like that, but Naomi knew this was definitely not either one of those.

"Tell us about it," Summer said gently. "If you feel up to it, anyway. We've been so worried about you."

"It was difficult," Naomi admitted. "There were good beings there, ones made entirely of light. They were warm and kind in their own way, but they couldn't always talk to me. And there were other creatures there, too. Dark ones. I did my best to keep away from them, but I could tell they were very strong."

"Did they want to hurt you?"

How could she explain something that took place in a completely different realm? Even the thoughts inside Naomi's head had been different, as though the language of her mind had been changed. "I don't really know. It was a very lonely place, I can tell you that. No matter how many other spirits were around, none of them were ones that I knew. There were a lot of them around when you pulled me back, though. I think the other beings there could sense the rift you created, and they wanted to see what was happening."

"Can't blame them there," Autumn remarked. "It sounds like it might be a holding place of sorts, for spirits who don't belong anywhere else. Like purgatory, if you will."

Naomi nodded, but the action hurt her head. "That would make sense. I'm glad to be back, but my body is so heavy. I'm not sure it was a good idea." It wasn't just her body that made her feel that way. It was something else, something her befuddled mind couldn't quite grasp.

"You're just not used to it yet." Leah smiled down at her. "You've been nothing but a spirit for several years now. You don't even know what gravity is anymore."

"I felt it." Naomi was only growing more and more tired, but it had been so long since she'd truly been able to talk to her friends. "When you would reach out to me, it was like a tiny hole had erupted in front of my face. It pulled at me, like Earth was calling me back, but I could never do anything about it. I put my energy into that window, but it didn't always seem to help."

"I'm sorry. That must have been very frustrating for you." Summer gently rubbed her arm.

"No, it's okay. It was good to know that you were still thinking of me, at the very least. I had no way of knowing how long I'd been there, because there was no such thing as time, but it felt like an eternity." There were no nights or days, just endless drifting. As heavy as her new body was, weighed down from the soil it had been formed from, she didn't miss the Otherworld.

"Listen, you really need to get some sleep. We all do." Autumn's eyes drooped a little at the corners. "We're all going to go home and give you some peace and quiet so you can get some good rest. We'll come back later this evening and have some dinner. Does that sound good?"

Naomi nodded. The others had offered her food shortly after she had come back, but her stomach was still churning from her transition. "Yes. It's been so long since I've actually slept. I'm not sure I even remember what it's like."

"Trust me. You'll enjoy it." They said their goodbyes and left the room, closing the door behind them.

Naomi could hear them chattering with each other as they made their way through the house and out the door. She stared up at the timber frame ceiling, trying to wrap her mind around the fact that she was back on Earth. It had been forever. As nice as it was to be back again, she wondered what it would have been like if the women could have brought her back to Charok. Was Julian still there? Did he still think of her? He had occupied her thoughts a lot since she had awoken, but she hadn't bothered to say anything about him to her friends. It's not as though they would know anything about him, and no matter how powerful their magic was, they couldn't reunite her with her true love on a distant planet.

Eventually, her eyes began to close. Light leaked in through the curtains, but she didn't care that it was still daytime. Just the fact that she was away from all the confusion of the Otherworld made her feel more comfortable than she had in a long time. She wondered if she would dream.

Just as she was about to doze off, she heard a noise. Her eyes flipped open and her hands reached out at her sides, but she had no weapons at hand. Maybe time had passed more quickly than she had realized, and Autumn and the others had already returned. But the slow and careful footsteps were made by only one person; that much she was sure of.

Her heart pounding in her chest, she slipped out

of bed. Autumn had lent her an old t-shirt and a pair of shorts, and they didn't seem like enough to protect her from whatever was coming. She realized that if she stayed where she was, she would be trapped like an animal. Naomi wasn't strong enough to climb out through a window, and her best chance was to make it to another door before the intruder found her.

Peeking out the bedroom door, she saw nothing. Naomi dashed across the hall and through an open door. She found herself in another bedroom—one that seemed to have been used for storage, judging by the stack of boxes in the corner—but there still weren't any outside doors there. With little option, she crawled under the bed and scooted all the way to the back near the legs of the headboard.

The footsteps had turned down the hallway and paused. Naomi held her breath, willing the stranger to give up and go away. But the bedroom door creaked open. She could easily see his feet as he stood in the doorway, probably surveying the room, trying to figure out where she was.

She held back a scream as he slowly stepped toward the bed. There was no other place to go. Whoever this was, he would get to her before she ever made it out of the room. Her friends had done so much work to bring her back, and now she would be gone again.

The interloper crossed the hardwood floor and stopped again at the edge of the bed. He knelt down, and when he peeked underneath the bed skirt, she could no longer hold back her scream.

"Naomi?"

6

Julian knew he shouldn't have broken down Autumn's front door. He could have just tried to call her, or even Beau. But the desperation that flooded his body was impossible to ignore, and he didn't have time to explain or ask permission. And now that he crouched there in an unused guest bedroom, seeing Naomi underneath the bed, he knew it had been worth it.

She had stopped screaming, and he reached a hand out to help her up. "It's okay. It's just me. But how are you here?" He wondered for a moment if he had gone crazy and he was just hallucinating. Or maybe it was just someone who *looked* like Naomi. But his body told him otherwise.

"How are *you* here?" Naomi was still the same as

she had always been. There was no mistaking those brilliant blue eyes and her dark, straight hair. Even a little disheveled and shaken, it was absolutely her. The touch of her hand was like fire against his skin, and as he pulled her to her feet, he could feel his wings burst through the skin of his back.

She responded in kind, her almond eyes elongating even further as her face stretched to a muzzle and her hair turned to a cascade of spikes along the curve of her skull. He watched with fascination as her wings unfurled, taking up half the space in the room. They were the most beautiful shade of blue he had ever seen, and she was an even more magnificent dragon than he had remembered.

Julian had been so fascinated with Naomi's transformation that he had barely noticed his own. The sensation was nothing compared to the way this woman made him feel and the animalistic urges she had been inspiring in him even before he had truly known that she was here on this planet. As unreal as it had seemed, his instincts were right. She really was back.

She studied him, her clawed hands reaching out to run down the smooth scales on his cheek. "It's you. It really is you. He said I would find you here. I didn't believe him, and it took so long that I thought he must have been wrong." Her voice was quiet, musing.

"Who?" None of this made sense. Just seeing her at all was confusing enough.

"Varhan. He's a wizard who helped me get to Earth. That's what I was doing when I left. He said the energies here would heal me. I couldn't tell you because I knew what it meant to have associations with one of his kind. Even if you understood, I didn't want anyone to blame you."

It had been so long since he had heard that name spoken aloud that for a moment, Julian didn't know who she meant. But a vision of the little round man in the middle of the woods soon came leaping to his mind. "Varhan. Varhan!? But I knew him. I worked with him all the time, even before you and I started seeing each other. I never would have been upset about that. It's because of Varhan that I'm here, along with three of my friends."

She smiled, a beautiful look on a dragon, and she reached out to touch his face once more. "He said that the spell to bring me here would change the lives of others. I suppose he meant you and your friends from Charok."

As suddenly as his heart had lifted at the sight of her, it fell like a stone into his stomach and all the fire in his chest quickly extinguished. She couldn't possibly know about Tazarre and the spell of poison, or the fact that all the other dragons on Charok were now dead, and he'd have to be the one to tell her. "Possibly. But right now, I just want to know how you got here."

Naomi nodded and looked up at him. "I lived here as a human for several years after Varhan sent me. The spell worked, and I felt much better. But it was lonely, especially because I was the only dragon here. Eventually, I made friends; I suppose you'll meet them when they come back. But five years ago, I was killed in a car accident and my soul was sent to another realm, a place unlike any I've been to before. But my friends hold special gifts and were able to use their powers to bring me back. Actually, I've only returned to Earth a few hours ago."

"I know your friends," he whispered. "There's so much that I have to tell you. It's going to take a long time of just sitting and being together." How could he explain that all the dragons on Charok had been purged and that he and the other men, along with the eggs they had snatched, had been the only survivors? It was more than she should have to hear about right now, but eventually, he would also be able to explain that her friends and his friends were all very well acquainted.

"That sounds wonderful." Naomi butted her head up underneath his chin. "For right now, just let me know that you still love me as much as you did when we knew each other before."

"Absolutely." He closed his eyes as he leaned toward her, her scales where he touched her smoothing out to soft skin. The waterfall of her hair showered across the back of his hand as he cupped the back of her neck, and he felt all the tension that had been building up in his body immediately dissipate as his lips met hers. He wanted to melt into her and become part of her, never having to give her up again.

Instinctively, his hands wrapped around her waist and lifted her up, pulling her close as he deepened their kiss. The raging instincts that had brought him to the house were now a craving in his veins, and he was finally getting to satisfy that craving after all these years. His fingers drifted underneath the hem of her t-shirt and up the smooth planes of her back.

Naomi's arms had wrapped around his waist, but she leaned back in his grasp to lift her shirt over her head. She hadn't been wearing a bra, which made sense since she had been wanting to sleep, and she revealed to him the pearlescent mounds of flesh that he needed so badly.

Julian laid her down on the bed. His mouth drifted down the hollow of her neck, slowly tracing the curves there, until he made his way to those gorgeous breasts. They were soft and sweet in his mouth, her nipples growing hard as his tongue flicked across them. Naomi groaned pleasurably and ran her fingers through his hair, pressing him harder into her.

This was so much more than Julian had imagined, even in his wildest fantasies. He had been so certain that he would never see Naomi again, yet he had allowed himself to envision what it would be like if he had. Now, having her right there in his arms and in his mouth, he wasn't sure he would be able to contain himself long enough to enjoy it.

"Oh, Julian," she breathed. "I've missed you so much."

"I've missed you, too." He was nuzzling her neck again. There was no square inch of her body that he didn't want to explore. "The other dragons I'm here with paired off with their mates, but I knew I could never do the same thing. There was only one woman in the universe for me." As he nipped her earlobes, his hands drifted down her long, lean body to the waistband of her shorts. Naomi arched her back as he pushed them away, making it an easy task. Her simple cotton panties came next.

Julian sat back on his knees to admire his mate. She was glorious in her nakedness. Her tumble of straight hair was dark against her snowy skin, the rosy buds of her nipples like delicate flowers on a teacup. Her waist tucked in underneath her ribs before the spread of her hips. Julian moved down toward the end of the bed, eager to explore the new frontier he had just discovered.

He ran his hands down her thighs as he gently pushed them aside, bending to kiss the delicate folds. She gasped and pulled away at first, but as his hands gently cupped her buttocks, she relaxed and spread her legs a little bit wider. He investigated her thoroughly, thrilled with the way she squealed and bucked underneath him.

"I want you," he heard her whisper. "Please, Julian. It's been so long."

These were the words he wanted to hear, and he instantly rose to his knees and maneuvered himself on top of her. She took him in with her body and with her soul as she wrapped her arms and legs around him and he sank down into her depths, the heat of her core blazing against him. He wanted to just stay like that forever, but his body had other plans. His hips moved, and hers easily picked up the rhythm. Their mouths and tongues entwined, and they were like one creature caught in a spiraling moment of ecstasy.

He felt her breathing come more rapidly as she undulated around him, suddenly even wetter and hotter than she had been before. He moaned into her mouth as he came, the years of loneliness and frustration exploding out of him as stars danced around the edges of his vision.

Afterwards, he lay next to her on his side, the back of his finger grazing against her cheek as she smiled up at him. "I know it's you. You're right here next to me, and you're the exact same person I've been dreaming about all these years. But even making love to you doesn't seem like enough to make it real. I'm afraid I'm going to wake up and find out that this has all just been an amazing dream." Julian didn't even want to fall asleep for fear that he would have to come back to reality eventually.

"I understand." She reached up to touch his hair. "I've spent far too many years wondering where you were, and if you were even alive."

With those words, Julian realized it was time to

tell her all the things she hadn't been around to see. "Listen, I need to share some things with you. I don't even want to, but it's not fair to leave you in the dark." Doing his best to give her a full account without focusing on too much detail, Julian told her of the War of Storms and how the wizards had jumped in with the ogres to fight against the dragons. He explained the spell that Tazarre had cast and why they could never go back to Charok. With a mix of hope and worry in his chest, he explained how he had come to be the foster father of Kaylee, how the other men had children of their own, and how her own friends' fates were intertwined with the dragons'.

By the time he was done, her pillow was soaked with tears. "I'm sorry that I've upset you, Naomi. I know it's a lot to take in, but you needed to know."

She nodded and wiped at her eyes. "I knew about some of this—vaguely. While in the Otherworld, I sensed that many of the dragons on Charok had been destroyed, and there was a group of dragons who had escaped to Earth, but I didn't know the entire story. And I didn't know that you were one of the dragon refugees." She took a deep breath and raised her eyes to the ceiling, blinking away her tears. "At least I have you, and that's more than I've had in a very long time. And I suppose, from what you're telling me, I'll have a daughter as well."

As much love as Julian had found in Kaylee and Naomi individually, it was nothing compared to what he felt at the idea of having them all together as a family. "Yes. You will. And I can't wait for you to meet her."

Naomi looked as though she was about to respond with something equally mushy, but the look in her eyes suddenly changed, hard and aware, her irises like blue stones.

"Julian. You have to get out of here."

"What? No. I'm not leaving you. Not for anything."

But she was off the bed and yanking her clothes back on, standing still as she listened. "You are. And now. There's no time to mess around."

Getting dressed himself, Julian reached out to her. "Naomi, it's been a long day. I think maybe you just need a little bit of rest."

She slapped his hand away. "No. You need to go. Now. It's for your own safety."

"But if there's some sort of danger, then I should stay." Julian, however, sensed nothing of the kind.

"Okay, okay." Julian finished dressing, wondering what he had done wrong. But it was clear that

Naomi wasn't in the mood to answer such questions. He would give her time. That was probably what she needed more than anything. "I'll leave for a bit, but I'll be back in a few hours, Naomi. I need you to know that. I love you." He desperately wanted to kiss her, but the sharp look in her eye stayed him. He left, feeling a heavier weight on his shoulders than he had felt in a long time. He did his best to rig the door shut so it would still be safe while he was gone and exited through the back of the house.

7

SHE DIDN'T WANT TO SEND HIM AWAY, BUT IF THERE was anything she had learned while she was in the Otherworld, it was to trust her instincts. Making love to Julian had temporarily blinded her to the potential dangers that surrounded them, and she had let herself believe that she was safe now that she was back in the physical realm of Earth.

But something was wrong with that notion. She couldn't tell Julian what it was; those instincts were still in that indecipherable language of the Otherworld. It didn't matter. She only knew there was trouble there, and she had to get him out of the way.

Now, completely alone once again, she stood still in the middle of the room. She heard nothing. Naomi shook her head and drew in a deep breath.

Maybe she had imagined it all, her mind unwilling to let go of the images that had danced before her eyes the entire time she had been gone. Being caught in that ether was like one long hallucination where nothing made sense, and she couldn't expect herself to come away from it undamaged.

Naomi made a silent promise to herself to call for Julian later—if she could even remember how to do that—and apologize to him. For now, she needed that nap she had been unable to get earlier. Padding back across the hall, she lay down, closed her eyes, and let her mind wander. Its first instinct was to think of Otherworld. She didn't know what the actual name for it was, only that it wasn't the same as any place she knew and loved. She felt the light and shadow that mingled there, a palpable substance around her that felt like swimming in a murky ocean.

Mixed with these images were ones of her and Julian back on Charok. These were the visions that gave her hope. She remembered how it felt to leap off the top of the mountains and let her body fall through the hot air until it was almost too late to snap her wings open. Julian had been right at her side during that daring stunt, the tips of his emerald wings just barely touching hers. It was a habit he had of always letting her know that he was right there. She hadn't needed him back then the way she did now. Naomi had been a young, confident dragon who—as of yet—had no reason to worry about life or what the future would bring. But still she had felt a certain sort of comfort in knowing she had such a sweet, steady love at her side. She let herself fall into the vision just as she had fallen in real life, with a wild sense of abandon.

But the back of her mind continued to fight her, and she was yanked back to consciousness. This time, she knew exactly what was going on. "I know you're there," she said to the air around her. The day was beginning to fade, sending long shadows across the floor, but there was another shadow in the room that she couldn't see. "I can sense you."

The response was there, but it wasn't an audible one. It was more like a deep rumble in the back of her mind, almost a laugh.

"You came through the portal with me." Her voice echoed in the empty house as she prowled down the hallway to the living room, certain she would find this other spirit soon. Its vibration was a familiar one that she had sensed in the Otherworld, but it hadn't been given a physical body in the same way that she had. Naomi wondered how it had survived, but that was a question for another time.

Another rumble sounded and she noticed a movement out of the corner of her eye, but as soon as she turned, it was gone.

"Leave here!" she commanded. "You don't belong. You're not from this place."

There was another flicker out of the corner of her eye, but this time she was careful not to look at it straight on. She followed it through the house, unsure of how to get through to this thing or even figure out exactly what it was. It moved faster as she pursued it, slipping through the pane of glass in the picture window at the front of the house and scuttling off into the growing darkness.

Giving up and tired beyond any sense of worry, Naomi went back to bed. This time, she actually fell asleep.

8

SHE HAD SENT HIM AWAY, BUT JULIAN FOUND THAT HE couldn't stay away for very long. He needed Naomi in the same way that he needed air or food, but perhaps even more desperately. She was like his very lifeblood, and knowing that she was once again on the same planet as he was meant that he simply couldn't live without her.

After picking up Kaylee, he drove back to Autumn's house and pulled up in the drive right behind Autumn's car. The three women were just getting out.

"What are you doing here?" Summer asked with a smile. "We've got some amazing news for you and the other guys."

"I know." Julian hated to ruin the surprise, and

he could see why they would be so happy to tell them that there finally was another dragon on Earth, but it was what it was. "I've already seen her."

"You have?" Autumn folded her arms in front of her chest, looking offended. "How?"

He did his best to explain, feeling a flush burn at his cheeks as he did so. Julian wasn't really in the habit of announcing his feelings aloud, and then there was admitting that he had broken into Autumn's house without her permission. "We're linked from our time on Charok, you see. I knew as soon as she came back. I mean, I didn't understand it, but I still knew. I could sense her presence, which I haven't been able to do in a long time."

Autumn gave a nod, Leah smiled, and Summer was jumping up and down and clapping her hands. "Julian! That's so exciting! I had no idea! Honestly, I didn't even think about her as a potential mate for you. I was just to happy to have her back."

He blushed a little harder. "So am I. And I can't thank you three enough for what you've done. But she doesn't seem to be quite the same. She was absolutely terrified when I found her."

"Most women would be if a man broke down the front door and charged into the house." She frowned at the splinters she noticed on the front step. "I wonder how many times I'm going to have to replace this thing."

He cringed. "Yeah...sorry about that. I'll pay for the repairs needed. But I have a feeling it wasn't my grand entrance that scared her." He could see her point, but in his mind, there was something deeper. "It was different. She got past it, and we managed to...spend some time together. But then it was like a switch was flipped, and she went right back into that defensive mode. She wouldn't even let me stay with her, insisting that it was for my own safety. It didn't make any sense, but I'm very worried about her." If what Naomi had told him was true and the three women had been her friends before she had died, then perhaps they knew her even better than he did.

Autumn reached out and touched his arm. "She's had a pretty crazy day, and even the last few years have been rough for her. Naomi probably just needs some time to adjust. I thought she seemed a little confused, myself. She mentioned something about there being shadowy creatures in the Otherworld, so that's bound to have affected her. Maybe there's something you can do to help reacquaint her with what normal life is like here."

"I've got Kaylee in the car, and I thought about picking up Naomi and bringing her back to my place for dinner. Just something nice and quiet. I don't think she's ready for a restaurant just yet." He would have loved to take her out to a fancy, romantic place with just the two of them, but for the moment, it would be simpler to go home and throw a few steaks in a cast iron skillet.

Leah smiled at him as she carried a duffel bag around Autumn's car and handed it to Julian. "That sounds like a lovely welcome-home dinner. She's also going to need a chance to go shopping for clothes, but us girls can help her with that. For the moment, I've picked up a few essentials and grabbed several outfits from my closet. Go ahead and take it with you."

He took the bag and realized just what all of this meant. He actually had Naomi back. It wasn't even going to be the same as it had been on Charok, because they wouldn't be sneaking off for secret dates. She would be living with him, or at least he hoped so. That wasn't even something they'd had a chance to discuss. There was so much to be addressed still.

When he made his way into the house, Naomi was just waking up. She still looked worn out, but she gave him a sleepy nod when he asked her to come back to his place for dinner. His heart jumped with excitement as he opened the back door of the car. "Naomi, I'd like you to meet Kaylee."

The light that had faded from Naomi's eyes was suddenly alight again. She instantly dropped to her knees and reached out to delicately touch Kaylee's hand. "Hi there, sweetheart. I've heard so much about you."

Kaylee grinned, her green eyes taking in every aspect of Naomi's face. "Pretty!"

"Why, thank you. I think you're very pretty, too. I hope that you and I can be good friends someday. Your daddy has asked me to come back to your place to have dinner. Would that be alright with you?"

The little girl nodded, reaching out with one tiny hand to gently touch Naomi's hair. It was a beautiful sight, and one that Julian had never thought he would get to see. Maybe things weren't going to be too difficult after all.

His love was quiet on the drive over, her body stiff in the passenger seat and her eyes watching everything carefully as they passed. At first, Julian speculated that she was just getting used to the sight of Earth again, but as they approached the other side of town, he realized there was something more to it. It was as if she were watching for someone. He opened his mouth to ask her about it and then quickly shut it again. Naomi would tell him when she was ready.

Arriving at his house, Julian's stomach crunched in on itself. He had no reason to really be nervous. Naomi probably wouldn't care too much about what his place looked like, and he knew there was plenty of room for both of them. It was a modern affair, very unlike Holden's big mansion or Beau's craftsman-style bungalow, but he had chosen it with the thought of a future family in mind. And if she didn't like the color of the walls or the floor, then he would gladly change it for her.

Still, there was something nerve-racking about the whole idea. It was as though he was a little bird and had built a nest just for her, but if she didn't like it enough, she might not stay. "I'll give you a tour first, so you know where everything is. I want you to be comfortable here. Then I'll start cooking."

Naomi nodded, and she looked in each room as he showed it to her, but she didn't seem all that interested. It wasn't until they reached Kaylee's room, right across the hall from his, that her eyes lit up again. "What a beautiful room you have, Kaylee," she said with genuine awe. "You must have a lot of fun in here."

The little girl wriggled in Julian's arms, and he

obligingly set her down. She toddled to her toy box and pulled out a doll, holding it in the air proudly as she brought it back to show Naomi.

"That's a very nice doll. Is she your favorite?"

At this prompt, Kaylee went to her bed and yanked down an old ratty teddy bear. Julian had bought it for her as soon as she had hatched, and it showed evidence of all the love she had given it.

Despite its appearance, Naomi readily took the teddy bear, gave it a hug, and handed it back to Kaylee. "It's absolutely lovely."

"Play?"

"Maybe in a little bit," Julian answered. "I've got to go cook dinner. You go ahead and play." He took Naomi by the waist and escorted her to the kitchen.

"You're smiling an awful lot," she noted.

He was glad to see the warm look in her eyes. It drifted in and out, and he had his concerns that she didn't really want to be there with him or that she was somehow disappointed in him, but then she would look at him like that again. "How can I not smile? You're here. I never thought I would see you again, and here you are in the flesh."

"Well, new flesh." Naomi looked down at her body. "It was a spell Autumn performed, since my original body had died. It felt strange at first, but I'm getting used to it."

"I think it feels quite nice." Julian waggled his eyebrows suggestively before turning to get the steak out of the fridge. "I had no idea you were so good with children."

"What do you mean?" Naomi took a seat at the breakfast bar where she could watch him make his preparations.

Julian shrugged and pulled a pan down from the rack. "You just seem to take so naturally to talking to Kaylee, like it's easier than having a conversation with another adult. I'm not complaining, I just think it's interesting."

Naomi looked down at the counter top. "I guess there's just less pressure. Seeing you again makes me happier than I can even explain, but it's also hard. There's so much explaining to do. I know there will be things to decide, and I'm not sure I'm ready to make any decisions. With Kaylee, there isn't any of that."

"She seems to like you," Julian noted. He knew they were all still in their honeymoon period, but at least they were off to a good start. "And as far as decisions, don't feel like you have to make up your mind about anything right away. We all understand that things have been difficult for you. I'm hopeful that you'll live here, but you can have all the time in the world to think about it." If he had it his way, he would have her under his roof and in his bed from there on out, but he didn't want to chase her off.

Her cheeks flushed. "I hadn't even thought about where I would live yet. Isn't that silly?"

"No. I think that just means you know you have plenty of friends here, and lots of options. I'm sure Autumn would be glad to let you stay at her place, as would any of the others." *But your rightful place is here with me.* He wouldn't say it out loud, but she knew he felt it.

Their conversation seemed to stagnate for a bit. Julian occupied himself with warming up the pan, tossing a salad, and browning dinner rolls in the oven. This wasn't anything like their experiences together back on Charok, and they had each spent their time on Earth separately. This was a situation unlike any he had been in before, so he tried to keep the conversation going by catching her up on everything that had happened since he had arrived.

"I'd really like for you to meet the other guys. You won't have much choice anyway, since they've all paired off with your friends, but I think you'll really like them."

"Oh!"

"What is it?" Julian turned to see Naomi staring off into the distance, but she looked surprised more than scared this time.

Her gaze slowly drifted to him and focused, bringing her mostly back to the present moment. "When Varhan sent me here, he said I would be changing the lives of others as well. He said three others would meet the ones they were meant to be with, and that I would be changing their lives for the better, even while I saved my own. Maybe he actually meant Autumn, Summer, and Leah."

Julian set down the pair of tongs he had just flipped the steak with. "That's interesting. That means he would have to have known that he would send the rest of us to Earth as well. Could it somehow have been all part of the same spell?" He had tried so hard to figure out just what Varhan had done to send them to Earth, but he hadn't known that Naomi was already there. Was that the part he was missing? Did it matter, since he knew they would never go back to Charok again?

"I always had a feeling that Varhan knew much more than he was willing to tell. He seemed so wise for his age, and the things he spoke of weren't typical to the ways of wizards. Granted, he was the only one I knew well."

Reaching across the counter, Julian wrapped his hand over hers. Naomi's fingers were long and cool, and they made the slightest movement upward to touch his. "I guess it doesn't matter, since we're all here now." He turned back to the stove, feeling a sense of peace and comfort that Earth had never afforded him before. It would be a process to get to know Naomi again, and to understand what she was like there as opposed to how she had been on Charok. It could even prove to be a difficult adjustment. But he loved her just the same, and they would get through it, no matter what.

9

Julian looked so comfortable there in his kitchen, cooking and talking as though this was something they did together all the time. It was nice, but in a way, it only made her feel more uncertain about their future together. He was confident that everything would be alright; he exuded it like cologne.

But she wasn't as certain.

Earth wasn't quite the same as she had remembered it. Naomi had never felt as though she completely belonged there, but she had never felt such a sense of impending danger before. Now, it was like she could do nothing but look over her shoulder. Julian had noticed, she was sure. How could he not after she had thrown him out of

Autumn's house? But he hadn't brought it up, and she was content to let the subject go for the time being.

There at Julian's, she knew she should have no reason to be scared. She pulled in a deep breath and focused on the sound of his voice, if not the words. Naomi felt that she needed something to keep her rooted there; something that would keep her from feeling as though she might float away if she didn't hold on just right.

"You should have seen Beau change a diaper for the first time. He was sure he could do it without any issues, but it didn't go so well for him." Julian laughed as he plated up a steak and turned around. His smile instantly faded. "What's wrong?"

Naomi's spine felt stiff. The apparition was back again. She hadn't seen it, but she could feel it. It lurked somewhere nearby, so close and yet so hard to see. Was it in her mind? Had she been seeing things? Reality was impossible for her to grasp right now. "It's here."

"What?" Julian's green eyes, which looked so much like Kaylee's, searched the room. "I don't see anything."

Her breathing was ragged now, as though the air had become too thick for her lungs. "I don't really know. I think something came through with me when Summer pulled me over from the Otherworld."

"What *kind* of something?"

"Something evil. Julian, it was in Autumn's house earlier today, and now it's here. You and Kaylee have got to leave!" With a sudden realization that nearly knocked her off her stool, Naomi remembered that she wasn't completely helpless in this situation. There had been long periods of doing nothing in the Otherworld, but she had also learned a few tricks to keep the shadow creatures at bay. She wasn't certain if they would even work there on Earth, but maybe she could try them.

"Now, hold on. I'm not going to leave this time, no matter what you say." Julian flicked off the stove with an angry gesture. "If there's some sort of danger here, then we're in it together."

"But you don't understand!" Naomi was on her feet now, a sense of panic expanding in her chest like a balloon. "Whatever this is, I brought it here. It's my fault, and I need to take care of it."

Julian came around the counter and took her by the shoulders, his eyes intense as he stared into hers. "You were alone for a long time. I get it. I know it's going to be hard for you to get used to it, but you *aren't* alone here. You've got me. You've got Autumn, Summer and Leah. Even though you haven't met them yet, you also have Holden, Beau and Xander. We're all here for you and for each other. If there's something going on, then we'll get everyone together and figure out how to handle it."

"I...I don't know if we can." The sense of dread that had been tingling against her spine was now a crushing pressure. Naomi turned to face it.

There was a small triangle of a shadow in the far corner of the dining room. To ordinary eyes, it probably seemed like an innocent enough space where the light from the fixture in the center of the room couldn't quite get past the china cabinet. But to Naomi, she knew it was more. As if she were willing it to life, the shadow began to take on a new shape. It bulged in the center, pushing upward and out into the light. It grew larger, the top of it forming into a head with wide shoulders. Soon enough, it reached all the way to the ceiling, a shadow so dark, it absorbed the light that attempted to bounce off it.

Naomi caught her breath as she took in the long, pointed horns that curled down on either side of its face and its slitted eyes. They were barely distinguishable from the rest of the form, only a slightly different hue of murkiness from the rest of him. He had less of a form as the shadow reached the floor, as though he had wrapped himself in a cloak of darkness.

"You see it now, don't you?" She pressed her back against the breakfast bar, putting her arm out to keep Julian from getting any closer to the creature.

But Julian showed no signs of seeing anything. "Naomi, we're completely alone. There's nothing here."

That deep rumble she had heard in Autumn's house was now a deafening thunder in her ears. "He's been here too long, and he no longer knows how to see things that aren't in physical forms."

"Who are you?" Naomi demanded. She had to get to the bottom of this.

"Who is who?" Julian sounded desperate.

The demon moved forward, sending a blast of cold air through the room. "I am the reason that there are no more of your kind on Charok. And I will be the reason that there are no more of your kind on Earth." His voice was heavy and low, like the sound of an avalanche.

"What do you mean?" But Naomi thought she already understood what he meant, she just hoped she was wrong.

"I am Tazarre!" the creature roared. "I paid the

ultimate sacrifice when I cast the spell that killed all the dragons on Charok, and now I'm here to finish the job."

Tears streamed down her face, but Naomi barely felt them. How could this have happened?

"Naomi? What's going on?" Julian was at her side, his thumb wiping a tear from her jaw. "Whatever it is, we'll get everyone together and figure it out."

"No!" She shoved him away. That was exactly what Tazarre wanted. If all the dragons were together in one room, and with the bonus of a couple of witches and a psychic, then it would be a walk in the park for this evil wizard to finish what he had started on the other side of the universe.

"You knew I was there," it growled. "You could sense me the entire time we were in the Otherworld. You should have done something about it then. But you were a weakling, just as you are now. Just as all your friends are. It will be simple enough."

No. It couldn't have been him; surely, she would have known if there was something that terrible with her. Everything in the Otherworld was jumbled and nonsensical, and it was nearly impossible to straighten it out and force it into the organization that Earth life demanded. And now that this thing was there and even Julian couldn't see it, she wasn't sure exactly how she was going to fight it off.

"Naomi? Please talk to me. Tell me what's happening."

"You're only going to think I'm crazy," she whispered. Naomi moved slowly away from Julian, testing the beast. It followed her with its eyes, barely even noticing that Julian was still in the room. She headed for the sliding glass door just off the back of the house, never turning away from Tazarre as she grasped the handle and pushed it open.

"Where do you think you're going, little dragon? My fingers have been itching to wrap around your throat ever since I came to the Otherworld." It glided forward on its shadowy, imperceptible feet.

"Then why didn't you do it then?" she challenged. "You were there. You know how it was. You could have killed me several times over." More than once, Naomi had seen figures of light fall to those of shadow. It was a distant, abstract thing, but still she had known what was happening. Such events sent a shiver of fear that made its rounds through all the innocents in the ether. Naomi stepped out onto the back porch, the warm air wrapping around her like a thick, suffocating blanket.

Tazarre laughed as he slid along in her wake.

"You already know the answer to that. If I had taken you then, I never would have had the chance to come here with you. I bided my time, waiting until the very last moment to attach myself to you as you went sliding back to Earth. Tell me, do your friends know what you've done for them?"

"Naomi!" Julian still stood by the breakfast bar, a desperate look on his face.

For a moment, she was terrified that he would try to follow her. The demon stood between the two dragons, his dark form taking up the entire doorway out onto the porch. She didn't want to know what would happen if Julian got too close to Tazarre. "Just stay there, Julian."

"I don't know why you're trying so hard to protect your little friend," the demon grumbled. "I'll come back and get him when I'm ready. But right now, my mouth is watering for you. I want to have your bones crunching between my teeth and your blood running down my throat." Tazarre was out of the house now, the two of them standing in the back yard.

If anyone was watching from their windows, they would see nothing more than Naomi slowly walking backwards down the path that led from the covered back porch to the main area of the backyard. They might wonder who she was, never having seen her at Julian's house before. They might even wonder why she was walking backwards instead of looking where she was going, especially in the dark, but they wouldn't see that she was trying to evade a demon. Even Naomi had a difficult time seeing him in the dim light. Julian insisted that Naomi wasn't alone anymore, but he was so wrong.

Part of her wanted to just fall to the ground in tears and give up. She had suffered for so long, constantly evading the darkness in the Otherworld and wondering if her presence there would ever end. It had, but she was no closer to being okay.

The other part of her, however, knew that she couldn't do that. She was responsible for Tazarre being there. She was the one who had endangered her friends and other dragons. At the very least, she could lead the phantom away from them. "If you want me, then come and get me."

Naomi finally turned her back to Tazarre. She felt the spread of her wings as her feet flew forward, lifting off the ground before she managed to complete her shift. Her partially-human body was heavy and awkward, and the absence of a tail threatened to send her headfirst back to the ground. But her legs grew shorter and thicker, her toes curling into claws. She felt the extension of her spine as her tail regenerated, swiftly compensating for the fact that she was already in the air. By the time she turned to look at the demon, she was not just turning her head, but snaking it around on her long, elegant neck.

Unwilling to let his victim get away so easily, Tazarre did exactly what she hoped he would do. Great dark wings expanded from behind him, filling up the yard as their feathered tips reached into the sky. He ascended with ease as he flew after her, a single wing stroke sending him rocketing through the air.

Naomi hadn't flown in a long time, not since before she had gotten ill on Charok. Earth had healed her body, as Varhan had promised, but now she could only hope that the new body she had been given would keep up with her demands. She faced forward once again, stretching her neck and tail and tucking her legs beneath her as her wings forcefully pumped through the air. "I'll sacrifice myself if it keeps him away from the others," she whispered to herself.

10

It didn't take long for the others to arrive. There had been no question as to where they would meet or just how urgent the matter was. Holden had heard the panic in Julian's voice, and now all the dragons and their mates were sitting in his dining room. It was well past bedtime for the children now, but they were all playing amicably in Kaylee's room. The steak dinner Julian had cooked had grown cold on the counter.

He did his best to explain what had happened. "I just stood there like an idiot, watching her fly off over the neighborhood. I didn't know what else to do. She was so insistent that there was something in the room with us, and she was even talking to it. By the time she left, I don't even know if she could hear my voice anymore." The others were sitting, but he paced the floor in front of the breakfast bar. He couldn't sit still as long as he knew Naomi was out there, possibly in danger—or possibly going insane.

"It's okay," Holden assured him. "We'll find her, and we'll figure this out."

"You said this was a demon?" Autumn asked, her eyes sharp. "Did she give it a name or say anything else about it?"

"Just that it had followed her here from the Otherworld." Julian wondered how things could have gone so wrong so quickly.

"Oh, no." The whispered voice had come from Summer, who had suddenly gone several shades paler. "I should have said something last night."

Autumn leaned across the table. "What?" she snapped.

Summer floundered, her hands moving through the air and her lips trying to find the words. "I never expected to be the one to go into the trance. We had all agreed it would be Autumn. But then I found myself just sliding down into that other world, like a hole had opened up in the bottom of my brain and I had no choice. I didn't mind, because as long as we got Naomi back, that was the only thing that really mattered. The drums were serving as a line to bring me back when I was ready."

"That all sounds pretty normal from what I recall reading," Autumn replied.

"Okay." Summer pulled in a deep breath and let it out slowly. "It was like I dove down into the Otherworld. Everything was thick and blurry, and there were shadows and light, just like if I was swimming in a pond with a bunch of shade trees over it. Naomi was like this brilliant burst of light, but there was darkness all around her. As soon as I grabbed her hand—or whatever you would call the equivalent of a hand in a place like that, since nothing has any real form—I felt something cold and icy against my spine. I just assumed it was a part of being there, and I didn't think about it at all. Not until we'd had some time to recover. I was going to ask Naomi about it when we got back to Autumn's house, but then we found out about her and Julian and everything just went from there. I figured there would be time later, once we were all rested."

"Don't blame yourself." Leah sat next to Holden, her face lined with concern. "None of us really knew what we were getting into when we brought her back. It was one big experiment."

Autumn was on her feet now. "There's no need

for blame," she agreed. "There's only time right now for action. We brought this thing into the world with a shamanic ritual, right?"

"Right," the other two women chimed in.

"Then maybe there's a chance that we can send him back with one." Her eyes were alight, and she was making a slow circle around the table as she thought. "Clearly, the trance that Summer went into was a powerful one."

"But dragging her back down into the Otherworld could be dangerous," Xander protested, his fist curled against the wooden surface of the table. "What if we lose her?"

"You won't," Summer promised. "Now that I've done it once, I know more about what to expect. I'll be in complete control."

"The rest of us aren't completely useless, either," Beau volunteered. "We've got plenty of firepower to attack him with. There's just the matter of finding him.

"I don't think that will be a problem." Ever since she had left, Julian had been resisting the urge to go flying off into the night sky afterward. It was only Kaylee that kept him from such a foolish errand, and he was grateful. It would be much better if he had his friends at his back. "I can find her."

Leah cleared her throat. "I took the liberty of calling the Rochesters on the way over here, just in case. They said they can come right over to watch the kids if we need them." The couple ran the local print shop and had always been sympathetic to both Leah and her psychic powers and the twins with their new age shop. They had met the dragons at a party last year, and they were now the closest 'normal' friends of the group.

Julian looked into the eyes of each of his friends and saw the same determination he felt in his heart reflected back at him. "It looks like we do."

THE SKY WAS BEGINNING to lighten. It would soon be morning, and people would be getting up out of bed and getting ready for work. Somewhere, out on the edge of town, someone might be stretching as she got out of bed, pausing by the window to admire the sunrise. She might be surprised to see four dragons go whizzing by her window, the early light reflecting off their scales. That would be a surprise enough, but it would surely be even more of a shock to see that three of those dragons had riders.

"How come we've never done this before?"

Autumn shouted over the wind to the gold dragon between her legs. "This is amazing!"

"Silly me. I thought I was giving you enough of a ride as it was," Beau retorted.

"Get a room, you two," Leah said with a giggle. She was perched on top of Holden, his red scales brilliant in the sun. But she looked as though she was enjoying this as well. After all, there wasn't much they could do until they actually found Naomi.

Summer was on Xander's back, her hands running slowly down his copper hide as though she was sending him messages through her fingers. Her head was tipped back and her blonde hair streamed out behind her. With her eyes shut, she looked as though she was already slipping into the shamanic trance they were all relying on. She had one of the drums strapped over her back.

Julian, flying solo at the head of the group, felt a bolt of loneliness in his heart. He'd had Naomi back, and now she was gone once again. The rest of the crew seemed confident in their ability to find her and save her from this beast that had followed her to Earth, but the only thing Julian really knew was that he couldn't survive without her once again. It would break his heart beyond the point of bearing.

He spread his wings wide, letting the wind lift him higher as they zoomed past the city limits and the trees underneath them began to thicken. Now that he was back in dragon form, he knew he had a better chance of finding her. Every sense was trained on her, listening for her heartbeat or the sound of her lungs, his nostrils flaring as they sought her scent, his very blood coursing only for her. If this was what the others had felt when they'd met their mates, then he almost felt sorry for them.

"Are we at least headed in the right direction?" Xander asked. They had made their best guess based on the orientation of Naomi's escape and the fact that she seemed to want to keep away from all the rest of them. It would be just as difficult to find her in a rural area as it would be to find her somewhere in town, unfortunately.

"I think so," Julian replied. He had been wondering if the faint clues of her scent that he'd caught had just been his imagination, but she was growing more solid in his mind as they left town. He closed his eyes, listening for her with every sense he had and letting his body do the work. He felt himself drift slightly east, and he didn't fight it. The others followed suit.

As the rural homes on smaller plots of land grew

into large farms and then dwindled into forest preserve, Julian felt the raw beast inside him suddenly come to life. His claws itched to dig into flesh, and he desperately wanted to burn down anything that got in his way. "She's close."

Swooping down in a dangerous nosedive, Julian picked up on her scent. It was heady, making him feel drunk, and he had to get to her as fast as possible. Once he did, he only wanted to scoop her up and take off with her, carrying her to some far-off place where they wouldn't need to worry about anything. But there was no such place on Earth right now, and they had work to do.

He landed with a thunk in front of a bluff. The rounded rocks created a sheer face tangled with vines and weeds. At one time, this edifice may have looked out over a lake or river that had long ago been lost. Julian headed forward even before he heard the others landing behind him. "Naomi!" he roared. "I know you're in there. You can't hide from me, and I want to help you."

A long blue muzzle poked out from the dark entrance of a cave. This side of the bluffs was still in shadow, the sun not yet high enough to reach down into the valley it formed. "Go away, Julian. You don't belong here."

He turned around. Holden caught his eye and nodded, urging him forward with a tip of his narrow head on his long neck.

"I do," Julian affirmed, still coming closer. He didn't think the cave could be very deep. If it was, Naomi probably already would have buried herself in it. "We're here to help you."

She thrust her head out all the way now, the deep blue stones of her eyes hard. "I left to keep you safe," Naomi yelled. "That thing is following me, and I'm the reason it's here. Now go away before it comes back and finds you all right here where it wants you."

Julian couldn't say he was unafraid of death, but at that moment, he would have gladly died at Naomi's side. "No one should have to fight their demons alone, and neither do you. I'm not going anywhere."

"Julian—"

"Don't bother trying to argue with me." He was at the mouth of the cave now, and he could just see the outline of her body in the darkness. "I love you, Naomi. You can't run from this thing forever, and you can't defeat it by yourself."

"But you don't understand," she insisted. "This isn't just some evil creature. This… this is Tazarre."

"What?" Julian's head snapped back slightly on his neck. That name wasn't one he had ever expected to hear again. "Surely, you don't mean—"

"I do. He told me that he was the one responsible for poisoning all the dragons on Charok. He was killed in the process, and that's how he ended up in the Otherworld. But he's here now, and the only thing he wants is to finish the job. I don't care if he kills me; I've already died. But I can't let him kill you, too."

The confidence he had been feeling drained from his system. Julian gestured with a wing for the others to join them, and he told them Naomi's news. "This is even worse than we imagined."

"It doesn't have to be," Autumn said stubbornly. "Knowing a thing's name actually makes it easier to take down, not harder. We just can't let ourselves be affected by that knowledge."

"That's easier said than done, for those of us who were there," Beau replied. "Tazarre is a thing of nightmares. We haven't even told the children about him."

"And with a little bit of luck, you won't have to." Summer, who always looked so peaceful and pleasant, jutted out her chin as she whipped the drum from her back and looked at the dragon in the cave. "Naomi, tell us where to find this thing."

"I don't know for certain, but I'm sure it will be back." Her wings shuddered against each other. "He's powerful, so much more than you probably imagine."

As if on cue, a darkness blotted out what little sunshine they had. It slowly slipped down the rockface, so massive that Julian had to take a step back to see the entire thing. It was no wonder Naomi had acted the way she had when the demon had shown up in his dining room; Tazarre was a terrifying sight. He'd been only a shadow to Naomi back then—and invisible to Julian—but now, he somehow had a depth to him that seemed infinite. As his massive form slowly descended down the bluff, the very oxygen seemed to be sucked from the air. "I can see him now."

"I see it, too," Holden gasped.

Tazarre bellowed a laugh like a collision of planets. "I've grown stronger. I'm getting used to this planet, and I think it suits me. Maybe once I'm done slaying your lot, I'll stay here and see what I can accomplish with the humans. I have a feeling they're a weak species."

An odd noise struck Julian's ears, and he realized

that Summer had started drumming. She sat on the ground at the mouth of the cave with her eyes closed and her hands moving rhythmically. Her eyes were closed, which was probably a good precaution.

Leah, who had been standing just behind Holden's wings, ran to her side with her own drum and joined in.

Tazarre watched them for a moment before he let out another roaring laugh. "Just as I suspected! Not only weak, but ignorant, too! At least the dragons on Charok had put up a bit of a fight and made things a little more fun." Two long shapes detached from the shadow and became arms with ghastly hands. They waved through the air, red sparks flying from their newly-formed fingertips.

"I don't think we have time to stand around and wait for the trance to start!" Beau shot into the air, puffing out his chest before unleashing a massive fireball. It struck the evil wizard and gave him only a moment's pause before he resumed his efforts.

Julian lifted himself on his wings. Holden was at the monster's face, filling it with a blasting heat, so Julian swung around behind. He pushed his body forward and his wings back, reached out into the air with his claws as he descended onto the back of Tazarre's head. He felt flesh under his grasp, but not like any other flesh he had encountered. It was cold and almost spongy, and the small amount of blood that spurted out of it was just as black as the rest of his body. Tazarre shook his horned head and sent Julian careening toward the cliff face.

Catching himself just in time, Julian rode the wind current up into the air and turned to look down. This was going to be a long and difficult fight.

11

Naomi shot forth from the cave, charging with her full strength. The men were in the air, but that gave her the perfect opportunity to fight from the ground. She tucked her head, slicked back her wings, and launched herself forward with every muscle in her legs and back. Slamming into Tazarre was like hitting the rock wall behind him, and it rang through her head and sent her reeling.

Naomi stumbled backwards and turned away from the demon to gather herself. Why did Julian have to show up? She was the one who had brought this thing into the world with her, and she was trying to protect him. Didn't he understand that? And bringing the other dragons along meant that Tazarre had them all together in one space, with a few bonus humans he could kill right along with them.

Summer and Leah were still beating away on their drums. Summer had a look of peace on her face, but Leah's brow was furrowed in concentration. Naomi recognized the sounds they were making; these were the same drums that had thundered through her soul as Summer was bringing her back from the Otherworld. She suddenly understood what they were trying to do, but she didn't think it was going to work.

She wound around then to Autumn, who stood just behind Leah and Summer with her hands out and her fingers spread. "He's too strong, and there are too many distractions. You'll never be able to drag him back there, and if you do, he'll keep Summer with him. We have to stop this and find something else to try."

Autumn kept her pose, but she nodded her head toward the other dragons. They were buzzing around the beast's head, blasting and tearing at him. The sun now filled the valley, making their metallic scales shine. They looked like robotic dragons, a wondrous sight if it were only under other circumstances. "They're giving him some pretty major distractions, and I'm sending my power to Summer to help her get into her trance. We'll get this done, Naomi. I know we will."

Naomi opened her mouth to protest, but she took a step back and realized what a magnificent scene she had before her. It didn't matter that she had ordered Julian to go away or that she had told her friends their efforts were useless. They were there for her, not just to protect their own lives, but to let her know she wasn't standing alone. Julian, in all his viridescent glory, was fighting for her just as he said he would. He was a gentle man, but he was a fierce warrior.

Still, red energy crackled between Tazarre's fingers. It grew, coalescing into a ball of electricity that steadily grew bigger and brighter. It was a horrifying image, but it brought the memory of a different one to the forefront of Naomi's mind.

She couldn't tell how long she had been in the Otherworld, because every second seemed like an eternity. Things moved differently there, including time. Her body was an unformed thing, floating in the murky world of ether that surrounded her. She was vaguely aware of the others, who came and went as orbs of lightness or darkness.

These, at least, were easy to distinguish. There were numerous shades of light beings, some brilliantly white and others a gentle glow, but the dark ones were nothing but the absolute absence of light. They hung on the fringes, waiting until they had the right opportunity. They gnashed at the light creatures with their teeth and broke them down, using them for fuel. Sometimes, when they had a particularly large or powerful adversary, they actually worked in teams. It was a horrifying thing to see the dark beings converge, but their cooperation only ever lasted for a short amount of time. Once their prey had been taken down, they turned to target each other.

Naomi had managed to stay out of the way at first, but it was only a matter of time before one of the shadow creatures noticed her. She could hear its thoughts as it approached, feel the hunger it had for her energy. It floated closer and closer, and she knew what fate she would meet. She'd seen it happen hundreds of times already, and now she would be the power that kept some evil creature alive. Naomi pulled all her energy inwards, terrified of what was about to happen, and when the being formed a gaping hole with which to eat her, a brilliant white beam of light shot it backwards.

Naomi looked, sure that she had been mistaken, but the black being was in full retreat.

After that, she did her best to pay attention to the

energy she emitted. It had come because she was scared, but over time, she learned to focus it and use it. The dark ones stayed away; perhaps they heard of her power. The light ones gathered around her, and so her time in the Otherworld was slightly better than it had been before. But even the 'good' creatures were still only near her because they wanted what she had.

REALIZING THAT HER PHYSICAL BODY, dragon or not, wasn't enough to maim Tazarre, Naomi sprang into the sky. She swooped between the other dragons, careful to avoid their swiftly beating wings. The others were building fire in their chests, filling up the special cavities within their reptilian bodies with the hottest flames they could generate, but Naomi was filing hers with something else. She pulled in all the energy, frustration and fear that this creature had caused. She added to it the pain and loneliness of being stuck in the Otherworld.

On top of that, she piled the sorrow of knowing that everyone back on Charok was gone.

As she swept into the fight, she balled it together and fired. The blast blew her backwards, her wings folding in front of her face. She could barely see, and she sped back with such velocity, she couldn't get her wings around to lift her weight.

Naomi fell toward the ground, watching in slow motion as a massive wall of white and blue raced through the sky toward the demon, spreading out like fireworks and cascading down over his head. Tazarre paid it little attention at first, instead knocking Xander aside as he tried to dig his teeth into the evil wizard's wrist. But where the dazzling sparks fell onto his obsidian hide, they burned down into his skin, sizzling away at his flesh and sending small plumes of smoke into the air. Tazarre writhed with the sudden shock of the pain, and the sphere of red that had been building between his fingers suddenly dissipated.

It was good. It was what she had hoped for. But still she couldn't gain control of her wings. She fell like a stone.

Until she was suddenly hurtling up again, strong arms around her middle. "I don't know what that was," Julian said from just behind her ear, "but I sure as hell hope you can do it again!"

"I can't," she gasped, suddenly realizing just how taxing that burst of light had been. "I can't do it again. I don't even know if I can stand up."

Julian set her down gently on the ground. His

claws clicked gently against her cheeks as he looked into her eyes, making sure she was alright. "You'll be fine. You have to be. We all have to be."

She watched him soar back into the air, her heart breaking all over again. What use was she if she was only good for one shot?

A cool hand, a human one, touched her shoulder. It was Autumn. "He's right. We must keep fighting, no matter what. Tell me how you did that."

"I don't really know. It was just something I used to do when I was in the Otherworld. I wasn't even sure if it would work here. And it took everything out of me." Her muscles felt as though they had turned to liquid.

Autumn's green eyes glittered. "If you can get yourself in the air and focus on what you need to do, I'll take care of the rest."

"But don't you need to help them?" Naomi looked over Autumn's shoulder to Summer and Leah, who still drummed away. The beats filled the air, though she had hardly noticed them while she had showered her light onto Tazarre. Summer's eyes were closed, but she didn't look as though she was in any sort of trance.

"I'll figure it out. I'm not sure how much good I'm doing her right now anyway, since she's still in our world. What we do know is that whatever you did seemed to work, and we need to expand on that. Just go, and don't worry about a thing." Autumn trotted back to the other two women, a bounce in her step.

Naomi knew she was right. Summoning the last of her strength, she pushed herself back into the air. Julian gave her a glance over his shoulder, clearly worried about her, but since she was in the air, he continued to fight. Naomi stayed a little back from the fray, trying to focus her mind once again. She felt some of that white energy building, but it wasn't nearly as much as she'd had before. Apparently, her first blast had left her with little to commit.

Just as she was about to give up and start fighting with her claws, she felt something crackle in her veins. It was a blue light this time, one that she didn't recognize as being her own. It vibrated through her blood and out into her muscles, building a shield around the cavity in her chest. With a grin, Naomi understood what was happening. Autumn was sending her energy to Naomi, just as she had promised.

Naomi closed her eyes for a moment, trying to summon that ball of light again. But it was hard to do with her friends being knocked around by the demon. Even more distracting was the thrilling sensation of Autumn's power in her own body. It was good to know she had friends, but it was almost too much excitement for her to bear.

A voice sounded inside her head. *Concentrate. You can do this, Naomi.*

It was Leah, reaching out with her mind and communicating with her. Naomi still heard the drums on the ground below, so at least she knew they hadn't given up their own plans just to help her. *I can't. I'm not angry anymore. I'm not even scared. I don't understand it.*

A tickle went through her mind that could have been a laugh. *It's because we're all here. That's okay. Use it. Use the knowledge that you're not alone. Pull your energy from us.*

I don't know if it will work! A volley of hatred and violence would probably be far more effective than one of love and joy.

Try it anyway, Naomi. It's at least worth a shot.

Naomi pulled in a deep breath and centered herself. She hovered in the air, relying on the other dragons to keep Tazarre distracted enough that he wouldn't go after her specifically. She expanded her chest as she pulled in all the love she had felt for Julian back on Charok. The friendship and fun she had found on Earth mixed with it easily, and it continued to grow as she concentrated on the intensity her relationship with Julian had taken on. The final topping was the new fondness she was just beginning to find for Kaylee, a sweet little girl who needed a mother and a friend, someone whom she barely knew but wanted to spend a lot of time with.

The energy crackled up through her throat and out her mouth almost without her own will. It burned in a pleasurable way as it sparked over her tongue, casting a light so bright and so white that it made even the sun seem dull.

Tazarre looked up, scowling at the new attack. He'd been building his energy once again, and he raised his hands over his head to keep the glittery orbs of light from landing on him. He spread his hands, creating a scarlet net with which to catch Naomi's light.

Her heart sank as she watched the first few sparks land on his net and stick. Tazarre laughed, and Naomi understood his intention. He would catch it all and throw it right back at them. Naomi had not only brought the demon there, but she had created the blast that would be the downfall of all of them.

But the sparks that had accrued on the net suddenly broke through, sending a deluge of

Naomi's blast right down into Tazarre's face. They sank in like napalm, burning away at his dark flesh. The smell of old ashes spread through the air, and the demon screamed. It was a horrifying sound, one that could be heard all over the valley, but it was a shriek that heartened Naomi and her friends.

While the evil creature writhed, Naomi snuck a look back at Summer. She drummed away, but her head was tipped back. Her eyes had rolled back in her head so that only the whites were visible. Naomi didn't know much of anything about what they were doing, but this must have been the same sort of trance that had brought her and Tazarre back from the Otherworld.

Newly inspired, Naomi gathered and sent another blast at Tazarre. It didn't have as much energy behind it; Autumn and Leah were concentrating on Summer now. But she could do everything in her power to keep him weakened. They had helped her, and she would do the same for them.

"No!" Tazarre screamed. "You won't send me back! You're too weak!"

But as Naomi circled around the back of his head to blast away, she saw that Autumn had lit a candle and set it between the drums. The flame was unusually big for just a small pillar candle, and the tip of it was beginning to spark.

She didn't know how to send her energy to the others as they had done for her. She had only ever been alone, but she whispered a prayer of hope and love on the breeze and hoped that it would reach their ears. In the meantime, she sent another explosion down on the back of Tazarre's head and watched as Julian and the others sent their fire blasting after it. The flames and the white spheres touched, detonating like a bomb and blasting a hole several feet wide in the evil wizard's shoulder.

The sparks over the candle flame had now turned into a small, swirling vortex. Naomi felt a bolt of fear run through her as she saw what was on the other side. It looked like nothing more than swirling colors, dark and light, indefinite and abstract. But she knew the hell of being in that place, a purgatory that no one should have to suffer—no one but Tazarre.

The bottom of the demon draped against the ground like a shadowy robe, but a corner of it suddenly picked up as though blown by an unseen wind. It tapered and pulled toward the vortex, slowly getting sucked in.

"You think you can defeat me? I'll take you all

with me, and then I'll pick your bones out from between my teeth as I eat you one by one!" Tazarre reached out toward Beau, trying to slap him out of the air. The gold dragon dodged to the side just in time.

But no matter how strong he thought he was, Tazarre was no match for what the women had done. Naomi's firepower had weakened him, and although his fingertips still crackled with crimson, he was slowly being pulled into the vortex. His arms fell to his sides and melded with the rest of his body, rendered useless. His great horns, which had looked so intimidating when he had first appeared in Julian's dining room, melted down into the sides of his head. His eyes, slits of red that had thirsted for her blood, sagged into his cheeks.

Summer and Leah pounded harder and faster on the drums. The vortex picked up speed, pulling Tazarre in. His shadowy form dragged along the ground as he struggled against it, but the force was too strong for him to resist. His blackness now filled the circle over the flame. Summer's body writhed, her hair dragging in the dirt. Autumn kept her hands out in the air near the vortex, protecting her sister from going in, too.

One last moan spilled from Tazarre's lips as his

body was pulled into the Otherworld, and the vortex slammed shut.

Xander morphed as he landed, running up on two legs to his mate. "Summer! Are you alright?"

She opened her eyes and gave him a beatific smile. "Of course."

A wingtip touched Naomi's and she turned to see Julian at her side; he looked tired, but victorious.

"Let's go home."

12

It was a beautiful morning as they made their way out of the forest and back to town. The sun was completely up now, and it illuminated all the beauty of the countryside below them. Naomi felt tears burn in her eyes as she surveyed the scene.

"What's the matter?" Julian, as always, was at her side, gliding beautifully through the air. "We did it, Naomi. We not only defeated him, but we got our revenge for what he did to all the other dragons back on Charok. We made sure that Earth is safe for the children. What's there to be sad about?"

She shook her head and touched her wing to his. "I'm not sad, I'm happy. I had forgotten how beautiful Earth was. Being here, and having everyone back, it's just too much."

"I guess you'll just have to get used to it," he said with a grin. He lengthened his body and flapped his wings, rocketing through the air toward home.

The others weren't far behind them when they landed in the backyard and shifted back to their human forms, and they all rushed inside to relieve the Rochesters of their babysitting duty. It had been late when the kids had finally gone to bed, and most of them were still asleep.

"Let's make sure we get together and have a big party," Autumn said as she walked in the back door. "But let's do it after we've all had some sleep and a hot meal."

"And a shower," Summer added with a wink. Her blonde locks were caked with dust from her trance, staining the ends of them a light brown.

When they had scooped up their sleeping children and headed off to their own homes and the Rochesters had been thanked a thousand times over, Naomi and Julian were left standing alone in the living room. Julian had checked on Kaylee, who was still fast asleep in her crib with her teddy cuddled at her side.

Naomi stood uncomfortably near the coffee table, not sure what to do with herself. She had been so happy on their journey back from the battle site, but now what? Everyone else would resume their normal lives, but she didn't even know what a normal life was.

"You were incredible out there," Julian said as he came back from the hallway. He took both of her hands in his. "How did you do that?"

"It's something I had to learn while I was in the Otherworld. I didn't even know for sure if it would work here. If it hadn't been for Autumn and Leah's help, I don't think I could have done it more than once." She tried to shove the memory of it out of her mind. It made her weary just to think about the process.

"It certainly did work. I don't think we ever could have defeated him otherwise. Summer may have pulled him through the portal, but I don't think she could have done that if you hadn't weakened him like you had. And the way that your fire mixed with ours? I don't think I've ever seen anything so beautiful!" They had been awake all night and fought all morning, but Julian was somehow still full of energy. He had let go of her as he spoke, pacing the floor and gesturing wildly with his hands.

Naomi couldn't help but admire him. He was so full of life, and that was one of the things she had always liked about him. Even when he was reading and studying, he did it with an air of enthusiasm that was contagious. It was just that energy, though, that made her wonder how he had managed to stay single all this time.

"Julian, I want you to know that I never expected you to wait for me, especially not for so long. I never thought I would even see you again." The words came straight from her heart and out her mouth, and she couldn't stop them. It was something that had weighed heavily on her mind since he had found her in Autumn's house, and it almost made her feel as though she didn't deserve him.

Julian paused, his hand in his hair. He turned wild eyes to her as his hand dropped to his sides, and he came around the coffee table. "Of course I waited for you. But don't make it sound like I did something heroic. I didn't even really know that I was waiting for you, because I thought you were dead. And I guess you were, at least part of the time. I just couldn't see being with anyone else."

"I understand." She looked down at where their hands were once again holding each other, their fingers intertwined. When she had met the other women and gone to parties with them, there had been plenty of men who had hit on her. She was flattered in a way, but none of them had the same sincerity in their eyes that Julian did. "I guess I'm still just trying to understand how we're lucky enough to be together again."

"Naomi, I love you. I'm so glad I get to hold you in my arms again, even if we had to cross the universe to do it. You mean more to me than you'll ever know, and I want to be with you for the rest of our lives. That is, if you want to be with me?" His eyes were soft, a liquid green with flecks of gold that swirled in his irises.

Her heart swelled, and that brilliant white light that had been her weapon was also her love as it swirled in her chest. She needed Julian, and it completed her soul to know that he needed her as well. "Of course I do."

Their lips met, and Naomi felt herself melting into him. She opened her mouth to let him in, reveling in the feeling of his tongue against hers. Her arms were around him, instantly pulling at the hem of his shirt. She needed him desperately. It didn't matter how tired she was or that they had just defeated a horrific wizard in the form of a demon, Naomi would never be able to rest until she had her man.

Julian seemed to feel the same way, and even as he held her and kissed her, he began walking toward his bedroom. No, *their* bedroom. As he reached the door, he scooped her up off the floor and carried her over the threshold. Julian flung the door shut with his foot and headed for the bed.

Naomi barely registered the California king-sized bed or the high thread count sheets as he set her down. Her mind was set on something else. She felt the cool air against her as he pulled off her clothing and ran his hands down her skin. It felt so good, but she needed more. Whipping Julian's shirt over his head, she flung it aside and reached for his belt buckle. She quickly revealed his member, hard and ready for her. Naomi sank down off the mattress and to her knees.

He had done so much to please her when they had met before, and now it was her turn. She took his length into her mouth, growing warmer at the moan that escaped from his lips. Her hands explored the hard muscles of his thighs, his narrow hips, and the curve of his buttocks as she sucked at him, eventually coming around to circle her fingers at his base.

"Oh, my god, Naomi!" His hands were in her hair, gathering it into a rough ponytail at the back of her head so he could see. "You don't have to do that."

"Yes, I do," she insisted, taking a break from her

work only long enough to argue with him. "I want to."

He tipped his head back as she pulled him in again, sucking his head all the way to the back of her throat. "As long as it's turning you on as much as it does me."

"Mmhm." She refused to let him go this time, and he understood what she meant. Naomi let her left hand slide down between her own legs, touching the firm bud of her clit. Julian had no idea how much it turned her on to do this for him, and she felt a tingle of excitement race upward from her core to her nipples.

Julian's hips pulsed gently, encouraging her. "I don't think I can do this much longer. I need you."

She sucked harder.

"Naomi, please. This feels too good."

She let him go, and he pulled her to her feet just so they could tumble down onto the bed together. They lay facing each other, kissing, exploring, touching. But Naomi wanted more, and she climbed on top of him.

He smiled in surprise. "It certainly seems like you know what you want."

"I do." She spread her legs and pierced herself on him, gasping at his girth as he filled her up. His hands cupped her buttocks as she slid back and forth on him. He was so hard, and she pushed her hips as far down as they would go, grinding against him.

Julian pulled her down so that their lips touched. She moaned into him, unable to control the waves of pleasure that suddenly undulated through her. He was hot and hard, and her walls pulsed against him.

She tried to pull back as he moaned his satisfaction, wanting the freedom of movement to give him the utmost enjoyment out of this. He was the most magnificent man she would ever meet, and she wanted him to know just how much she appreciated him. But he had other ideas, and he kept his hands cupped over the back of her skull so that he could continue to kiss her. Just as his cock was buried in her, he buried his tongue in her mouth. Their hips bucked and pulsed, clamoring against each other as they found their climax. Naomi's scream was only stifled by their kiss and she felt his circumference grow in response.

But to her surprise, Julian wasn't done with her just yet. He rolled her over so that he was on top, sinking his shaft just a little bit further inside under his weight. Their bodies were glued together, and she surged around him once again. He plowed her into the mattress, the headboard bumping against the wall. Naomi squealed as the spasms racked her body once again, making her twitch down to her toes. Julian finally broke their kiss and buried his face into her neck as he came with a roar.

Julian held her in his arms, their legs tangled together as he pulled the blankets over their naked bodies. She rested her head against his chest, feeling completely satisfied and yet knowing that she wanted him even more than she had before. She would never get enough of him, and that was just the way it should be.

13

EPILOGUE

Julian smiled as he landed in the back yard, turning to watch Kaylee. She was just getting used to her wings, since he had spent a lot of time encouraging her to remain in human form. But he had someone to help him in the sky now, and the three of them loved taking evening flights. Kaylee was always impatient for the sun to go down, bouncing in joy as she waited for the right time. And she always slept very well at night afterwards.

The little dragon spread her wings and tipped them upward, trying to slow herself down. She was coming in too steep, which was usually her problem. Naomi was right at her side, touching the tip of her wing to the little girl's. "Keep flapping, dear. You need a little more lift!"

Kaylee obediently swooped back up as she slowed down, landing lightly in her father's arms. She screamed her excitement. "Again! Again!"

"No, sweetie. It's about time for bed. You need to get your rest so we can go again tomorrow. And maybe we can go even further." He watched as Kaylee shifted back to her human form in his arms, her wings tucking into her back and folding away. Her scales each stood on end and flipped over, rippling down to soft skin.

"Yes, it's definitely time for bed," Naomi agreed. Her wingtips touched the ground as she walked toward the back door, and she shifted more slowly than usual.

"Are you alright?" Julian had noticed that she'd been tired a lot lately. He had chalked it up to the fact that she was still getting used to being on Earth, plus the fact that they had a little one to run after all day. Kaylee was energetic, and she could be a lot to keep up with.

She shrugged, now completely back to a form that was acceptable by society, should any of their neighbors happen to look out the window and see her profile in the porchlight. "I'll be fine. I didn't sleep very well last night, so I think I'll turn in early."

Julian nodded. "You go ahead and get ready for

bed. I'll give Kaylee her cup of milk and her bath." He didn't mind being the one 'stuck' with bedtime duty. He enjoyed the quiet moments with his daughter, when he could wash her hair and talk to her about the events of the day. She was getting bigger all the time, constantly learning new words and showing him new things she could do. He didn't want to miss out on any of it.

When he had her all clean and dressed in her pj's, he carried her to bed. She could walk very well on her own now, but there was nothing better than snuggles from a freshly-bathed child. He sat in the rocking chair and pulled a book from the shelf. "How about this one? We haven't read it in a while."

Kaylee nodded her agreement, and he began reading about a little puppy who couldn't seem to stay out of trouble. Julian flipped the pages slowly, knowing that she needed to get to sleep, but was unable to resist this wonderful, special time with her.

His reading was interrupted by a thump against the wall. "Naomi? Are you alright?"

"I'm fine!" came the muffled reply.

Julian read two more pages before he heard a crash. He gathered Kaylee from his lap and set her in her crib before dashing out of the room and across the hall. "Naomi!" But when he grabbed the bedroom doorknob, it was locked. "Let me in!"

"Hang on!" There was more crashing and a gasp that sounded pained.

"What's going on in there?" The dark fantasies that occupied Julian's mind were a scary thing. Had another demon shown up, one they didn't know about? Was there some other enemy, perhaps a neighbor who had seen them in dragon form?

"Just a sec!"

The next few seconds were painfully silent, and then Julian heard the click of the lock. He rushed in to see Naomi standing demurely at the end of the bed, a smile playing on her lips. Several books had been knocked off a nearby shelf, and a porcelain lamp lay broken on the floor. "What happened? Are you alright?"

"I am," she nodded. "It turns out we don't have quite enough space to shift indoors."

He felt completely stupefied as he looked at her. "But why would you do that? We just spent over an hour with Kaylee as dragons."

Naomi looked down at the floor for a moment before lifting her eyes to meet his. "There are some things I just can't do as a human."

"Like what?" he asked slowly. "Naomi, you're really starting to make me worry."

She reached out and took his hand, leading him around the bed and pointed to the floor. On a pile of blankets lay a shimmering silver egg. Julian stared at it for a long moment, his brain refusing to acknowledge what he was seeing. "Is that...?"

Naomi beamed at him. "Yes. Now I know why I'd been so tired and why I hadn't been able to sleep. I'd never gone through this before, so I had no idea what to expect. But as I was about to change for bed, I had this overwhelming sensation to shift. I couldn't stop it."

Julian knelt down to touch the smooth shell. It was just like the egg Kaylee had come out of, but larger and more robust. And it was his. Truly his, and Naomi's as well. He felt a tear trickle down his cheek. "It's absolutely beautiful." He stood and pulled her into his arms, kissing her.

"So, you're happy?" she asked when they finally broke apart.

"More than you could ever know." He didn't even know quite how to put it into words, but they were going to have a child together. Another dragon would soon be hatched on Earth. Not only would they be expanding their family, but extending a race nearly brought to extinction by genocide. Only time would tell if future generations would keep the line going, but at least for now, they had one more soul to love.

Julian squeezed her hands and let go. "I think we've got a sleepy little girl in the next room who would love to see this." He slipped back across the hallway.

Kaylee was standing in her crib, leaning on the rail. She watched her father come in the room with wide, curious eyes. "Story?"

"We'll finish in a minute, I promise. But first, I've got something exciting to show you." He picked her up and took her back to the master bedroom, smiling at Naomi as he did so. "Look right over there. You're going to be a big sister!"

She pointed one chubby finger at the shape on the floor. "Egg?"

"Yes, sweetie." Naomi took Kaylee now, wrapping her in a big hug. "We're going to have a baby."

Kaylee clapped her hands. "Baby! Baby!"

Julian held his mate and his daughter, staring down at the silver egg that would bring their family and friends incredible joy. He had left so much behind on Charok, but there on Earth, he had found so much more.

ALSO BY MEG RIPLEY

ALL AVAILABLE ON AMAZON

Shifter Nation Universe

Special Ops Shifters Series

Werebears of Acadia Series

Werebears of the Everglades Series

Werebears of Glacier Bay Series

Werebears of Big Bend Series

Dragons of Charok Universe

Daddy Dragon Guardians Series

Shifters Between Worlds Series

More Shifter Romances

Shifters of the Elements Series (cowritten with Lark Sterling)

Shifter Daddies Collection

Beverly Hills Dragons Series

Dragons of Sin City Series

Dragons of the Darkblood Secret Society Series

Packs of the Pacific Northwest Series

<u>Early Short Stories</u>

Mated By The Dragon Boss

Claimed By The Werebears of Green Tree

Bearer of Secrets

Rogue Wolf

ABOUT THE AUTHOR

Meg Ripley is an author of steamy shifter romances. A Seattle native, Meg can often be found curled up in a local coffee house with her laptop.

Download Meg's entire *Caught Between Dragons* series when you sign up for her newsletter!

Sign up by visiting Meg's Facebook page: https://www.facebook.com/authormegripley/

Printed in Great Britain
by Amazon